Saving the CEO

THE KENDALL FAMILY
BOOK ONE

LIWEN Y. HO

Saving the CEO

Copyright © 2023 by Liwen Y. Ho. All rights reserved. No part of this publication may be reproduced, distributed, or transmitted in any form or by any means, including photocopying, recording, or other electronic or mechanical methods, without the prior written permission of the publisher, except in the case of brief quotations embodied in critical reviews and certain other noncommercial uses permitted by copyright law.

This book is a work of fiction. Names, characters, places, and incidents either are products of the author's imagination or are used fictitiously. Any resemblance to actual persons, living or dead, events, or locales is entirely coincidental.

ISBN: 9798391176916

Cover Design: Kristen Iten

❀ Created with Vellum

To younger siblings who go through life with big footsteps to follow and their older siblings who leave them behind.

CHAPTER 1
Devin

The last thing Devin Kendall had time for was finding a wife. Running a multimillion-dollar empire and keeping an eye on his siblings? He had enough on his plate with those responsibilities alone.

"What was Grandfather thinking?" he mumbled out loud to an empty office. The overcast sky he saw outside the large windows matched the somber tone of his voice. He'd come up against a lot of problems in his thirty-five years of life, but none had seemed as unsolvable as his current situation.

He rose from his chair and began pacing the length of his office with his phone in hand. The text he'd just received from his cousin Nick stared back at him, making his jaw clench.

Hey cuz, just a friendly reminder you have three months before you hand the biz over to me. Enjoy them while you can.

Three more months. He had approximately ninety days until the start of the new year, which was when he was expected to hand over Kendall Industries to his obnoxious younger cousin. Nick would no doubt turn around and sell the automotive parts manufacturing company to the first available buyer, then take the money and squander it.

Devin couldn't allow the business that had been in their family for three generations to fall into the wrong hands. But he also couldn't save it, not in his current state. His grandfather's will stipulated that the company could only be owned by a Kendall who was married. There was some antiquated reasoning behind the request—one he didn't pretend to understand—and he had no choice but to accept it.

Since his grandfather's passing last year, they'd had a grace period in which a subsequent heir could be named. In that time, Devin had been promoted from COO to acting CEO. But it was only a matter of time before he'd lose his position. His bare ring finger, and even emptier social calendar, put him out of the running. While most of his cousins qualified to inherit the business, none of them had shown any interest in taking it over—until Nick eloped last month and threw his hat into the ring. Since then, he'd made his intentions to unseat Devin as annoyingly loud as possible.

The question now was how soon could Devin find a woman who'd be willing to marry him?

"Hi, big bro!"

The feminine voice calling out to him from the doorway stopped him midstep. He greeted his sister with a curt nod. "Bekah, what brings you here?"

She gave him a sugary sweet smile that made his suspicions rise. "I'm just grabbing lunch with a friend downtown and thought I'd stop by and see how you're doing."

He returned to his chair behind his large mahogany desk and gestured for her to take the seat across from his. It wasn't the first time Bekah had dropped by unannounced and, knowing her, it wouldn't be the last. They shared their father's light brown hair and their mother's blue eyes, but their personalities were like oil and water. She thrived on spontaneity and had only recently settled on a career path at the age of twenty-five. He could never predict what rabbit hole Bekah would go down next, but one thing he could be sure of: she was here to ask for money. "How much do you need, sis, and what do you need it for?"

Bekah's cheeks reddened. She placed her hands on her hips, her fingers digging into the hem of her sweatshirt. "Can't a girl come and see her brother without having some kind of ulterior motive?"

"Yes, but I've yet to see it happen." Devin glanced at his watch, noting the time he had left before his next meeting. "You have exactly eight and a half minutes to present your case—starting now."

"Okay, fine, there is something I've been thinking about. Now, hear me out ..."

Devin bit back a knowing smirk. If he had a dollar for every time he'd heard that line from his sister, he'd have enough money saved up to buy his dream car. It wasn't that he couldn't afford the latest Porsche with his current salary, but he'd been trained at a young age to count every penny. Every second mattered as well. Their father had drilled the strictest work ethic into him. Being the oldest child meant carrying more responsibilities and burdens. Was it fair? Not really. But he was thankful that he had been the one to bear the brunt of their father's discipline rather than his siblings.

"What do you think, Dev?"

Devin blinked. It took him a second to realize Bekah was waiting for him to answer. He steepled his fingers together and pretended to consider her words. "What do I think? It sounds interesting."

Bekah wrinkled her nose in exasperation. "Devin! You weren't listening—again! How do you expect to ever find a girlfriend? Don't you know that no woman wants to be ignored? We want to feel like the center of a man's universe. We want to be heard and validated and made to feel important. When are you going to understand that?"

"All I understand is that kind of mentality places a lot of

expectations on one person and does not sound healthy for either party."

He loosened his tie and yanked it off. After tossing it onto his desk, he ran his hands through his hair. All this talk of the opposite sex had him feeling cornered like David must've felt in front of Goliath. Maybe his sister was right. He could handle board meetings and negotiating high-stakes contracts for work, but he was clueless when it came to women. He'd never met one who held his attention long enough to pursue anything serious. What he wanted was someone business-minded who understood his drive and ambition and wouldn't constantly be in need of attention. A woman independent enough to have her own goals and dreams and not let her life revolve around her husband.

"I'm just trying to help." His sister's tone softened as she continued, "What's not healthy is you working all the time. When was the last time you went out?"

"I had that work event over the weekend."

"For *fun*."

He opened his mouth to answer, then shut it again. The knowing look on her face made him balk. "I don't need to have fun."

"I beg to differ! This is one area that you could really use some help with, and I know just the person to help you."

"I don't have time—"

"Hear me out, Dev."

"My next meeting's at eleven thirty."

Bekah pulled out her cell phone and held it up for Devin to see. "I still have two more minutes."

"Fine, but make it quick."

"Great!" She flashed him a genuine smile for the first time that morning. "What you need is a woman in your life, someone who will help you have some work-life balance. And I know exactly how you can find one."

"I don't need help in that area," he uttered through gritted teeth. "I can easily find a woman—or ten—to date if I want to. *I'm* not the problem. The problem is that dating is a waste of time. Who has the luxury of going to dinner and the movies every night? My schedule doesn't allow for that. There should be a more efficient way, one that skips over the mundane, drawn-out process of getting acquainted. What I need is to be paired up with someone who I already know is compatible with me."

Her eyes widened. "Whoa, who are you and what have you done with my big brother? This is the first time I've ever heard you talk like this! You sound like you wouldn't mind having a girlfriend."

Actually, what he needed was a wife, but his sister didn't know that. Since he had handled all the business affairs related to their grandfather's will, he was the only one of their siblings who understood the gravity of the situation. He kept his tone nonchalant as he replied, "I figure I'm not getting any younger. It's about time I settled down."

Bekah stomped her feet and let out a high-pitched squeal. "This is awesome! Scarlett's going to be thrilled!"

Devin furrowed his brows at this unfamiliar name. "You're not trying to set me up with one of your friends, are you? I'm not interested in twenty-somethings. I need someone who's serious about commitment."

"And you're going to get one!" She clapped her hands in excitement. "Scarlett *is* my friend, but she's not the one you'll be dating. She's the matchmaker."

"The what?"

"Matchmaker. Her family's been in the Christian matchmaking business for three generations. They're looking to expand and reach clients in the corporate world, especially people who have packed schedules and are too busy to date. She asked if I knew anyone who would benefit from their services, and you were the first person that came to mind!"

His eyes widened in disbelief. "You're serious?"

"Totally serious! Scarlett is amazing at her job. She's had a perfect track record of putting compatible people together. All the couples she matched are still married. One even named their dog after her."

"Their dog? If you're trying to reassure me of her credentials, you need to come up with something a lot more convincing."

Bekah groaned. "Why do you have to always be such a grump? If Scarlett weren't so desperate, I would totally find someone else to introduce to her."

"I don't know if you're listening to yourself, sis. Telling me that your friend is desperate makes it sound like she's not able to find clients because she's not good at her job. Is she or is she not a good matchmaker?"

"She's the best! She's only desperate because she's in a competition with her sisters to see which one of them can sign their first corporate client and find a successful match for them. She's in it to win it."

Devin's ears perked up. Her friend sounded hardworking and determined—two traits he appreciated in a person. He could get behind someone like that. "What happens if she loses?"

The room grew silent as Bekah chewed on her lower lip. Concern clouded her eyes as she sighed. When she finally spoke, her voice was soft and somber. "Whoever loses has to shave off one of her eyebrows."

His jaw dropped. Laughter rose from his chest and tumbled out of his mouth. His shoulders shook as he tried to catch his breath. All this drama over an eyebrow? This was so ridiculous; he couldn't stop laughing.

"This isn't funny, Dev!" Bekah insisted. "It's about more than an eyebrow. It's a matter of honor. Scarlett's the youngest of four, and she's always having to prove herself to her older sisters. Winning this competition will help her earn their respect. And it would be nice, of course, if she could keep both of her eyebrows. She has the most perfectly arched brows you've ever seen!" She scrolled through her phone for a few seconds, then passed it to Devin. "Look at them!"

He studied the photo she had found. Two women wearing bright green goo on their faces looked back at him. He recognized the one on the left as Bekah and presumed the other one to be Scarlett. Placing his fingers on the screen, he zoomed in on the woman to the right. Her dark brown hair was pulled back by a headband with cat ears, allowing him to see her well-groomed brows and her eyes. Piercing green eyes that captured his attention and made it hard to look away. There was also something about her smile. It radiated joy and warmth and awakened a curiosity in him.

She appeared to be content and fulfilled—two things that continued to evade him in life. Perhaps she did have knowledge that he could benefit from. Moreover, he was in a position to help her win a family battle. It wasn't on the same scale as his, but he understood the pressure all the same. If they could be of mutual assistance to one another, it made sense for him to agree.

He met his sister's gaze and nodded. "I'll do it. I'll sign up to be her client."

CHAPTER 2
Scarlett

"You showed your brother *that* picture?!" Scarlett shrieked so loudly the older couple sitting at the next table stopped talking. Eyes wide, they held their forkfuls of pasta midway to their mouths and glanced over. Smiling sheepishly, Scarlett apologized in a hushed voice, "Sorry! Everything's fine!"

"Are you sure you know which one I'm talking about? Let me show you." Bekah rummaged through her bag, groaning in frustration. "Great. I think I left my phone at Devin's office. It's the one we took at your place last month when we had our girls' night in. I thought we looked so cute."

"We did. It's a fun picture and we had a really good time that night." Scarlett swallowed her disappointment and tried to sound gracious. If there was one word to describe the friend she'd met through her church's women's group, it was *innocent*. It was hard to be upset with someone who didn't have a mean bone in her body. Not to mention the fact that Bekah had gone out on a limb for her by talking to her brother. "I was just hoping that your brother's first impression of me would be more of a professional one. One that makes him think *successful matchmaker* when he sees me, not The Incredible She-Hulk."

"Oh, that's a good point. I didn't think about that." Bekah furrowed her brows as she brought her glass of water to her lips. Looking thoughtful, she took a long sip. "I don't think the photo left a bad impression though. Devin started to smile the longer he looked at it. If there's anything you should know about my brother, it's that he *never* smiles. And when I told him about the bet you have with your sisters, he laughed! I can't remember the last time I heard him laugh like that."

Scarlett cringed. "You told him about the bet? Why did you tell him about that?"

"I wanted him to know why you need his help so badly. He's extremely competitive, so I knew he'd understand if he knew what was at stake."

Scarlett rubbed her temples and forced herself to breathe. Could the situation get any worse? Not only did Bekah's brother think she was unprofessional, but he also knew she was desperate, too. He probably assumed she and her sisters were immature for coming up with such a silly punishment. Which, to be honest, they sometimes were, but at least they knew how to have fun. Thankfully, he hadn't been dissuaded from signing up for her services. That was a big win. And now she was one step closer to winning the bet. From here on out, there was nowhere to go but up. That's what her Nanna used to say.

A dull ache spread through her chest. Oh, how she missed her grandmother. It'd been a long and lonely year since she went to be with Jesus. Scarlett not only missed her Nanna's homemade pies but more so her words of wisdom and encouragement. She'd been the one person Scarlett could confide in about her insecurities and fears. And the only person who had never compared her to her sisters or made her feel less beautiful, talented, or accomplished than them.

Without her Nanna around, Scarlett had to work hard at reminding herself she was more than the baby of the family. That she was no longer the little girl who could never keep up with her sisters' longer and faster strides. This was the year that she vowed would be different. She'd just turned thirty. A new decade was sure to bring with it new adventures. Maybe she'd even start thinking seriously about pursuing her dream career full-time. She just needed to keep putting her trust in God and doing her best. That was another thing her Nanna used to say.

Shaking off her doubts and worries, Scarlett reached over the table and squeezed Bekah's arm. "Thank you for trying so hard to help me. I really appreciate it."

Her friend's blue eyes lit up with relief. "Of course! You're like the older sister I never had but always wanted."

"And you're the younger sister I always prayed for. I'm so glad God brought us together."

"Me, too. I can't wait for our next girls' night in. I just bought a new facial mask that has real rose petals in it. It's a nice honey color, too, and smells divine."

"That sounds a lot less lethal than Hulk green," she replied with a laugh. "I'll check my calendar and let you know when I'm free."

"Sure thing! We can do it at my place this time."

Their server, a young man in a black vest, stopped by to deliver their lunch. Once they had said grace, Scarlett pushed up the sleeves of her pink zip-up hoodie, ready to dig into her meal. The delicious scents of lemon, garlic, and butter wafted up from her bowl of lobster ravioli. Across from her, Bekah took a generous bite of her lasagna.

For a minute, Scarlett let go of her worries and let herself savor the moment. The delicious flavors of her food, the hum of conversations going on in the restaurant, and the busy streets outside their window of downtown Mountain View. Mondays tended to be busy, but since she had the day off, she'd packed her schedule even tighter than usual. Dance class first thing in the morning, then dropping off coffee for her sisters at the office before volunteering at the local animal shelter. This was the first time she'd sat down today.

So much for learning to slow down.

She'd been trying to be more of a Mary than a Martha since her Nanna had passed. If there was one regret she had in life, it was not enjoying the time she'd had with her grandmother when she'd had the chance. She'd always been too preoccupied with something, either school, dating, or work. What she really needed to prioritize now were the relationships in her life.

Starting with the friend she was blessed to be spending time with. Scarlett turned her focus back on Bekah.

"I hope it won't be too hard for you," Bekah piped up in between bites, "to find a woman for Devin. I love my brother, but he's not exactly the most interesting guy."

"What do you mean?"

"He wears the same outfit every day—a white dress shirt with black slacks and a tie in some shade of blue. He hardly ever goes out for lunch and lives on microwaveable frozen meals at the office. And his idea of fun on the weekends is organizing his old CD collection."

"Really? You must be exaggerating—oh, you're not," Scarlett corrected herself when she spotted Bekah's pointed look.

"I wish I were. Devin got all the calm, boring genes, and my other brother, Jace, got the fun, exciting ones."

"Jace is a rock star, is that right?"

"Yes. It's so strange to think how different they are, considering they're supposed to be identical twins."

"That's amazing when you think about it," Scarlett mused. "There are billions of people in the world and God made every one of them with such distinct personalities, even two people who share the same DNA. I'm looking forward to meeting Devin and learning more about him."

"Don't expect too much. He's not someone who's full of surprises."

"That's okay. The fact that he's consistent and predictable will be an advantage in finding him a match. Plenty of women, especially those in their thirties, are attracted to guys like him. They want someone who's dependable and reliable and done playing the field."

"That's Devin all right. Although he never really played the field to begin with."

"Has he had any long-term relationships?"

"Not that I know of. Jace is the one who hung out with a different girl every week. Sometimes he'd drag Devin to go out with him, but Dev usually came home early. Jace has always been the party animal and Devin the party pooper." Bekah's expression became solemn as she set down her fork. "Maybe you should look for someone else to be your client. I don't want you to go to all the trouble of setting Devin up with different women when it's not going to work out with any of them."

Scarlett couldn't help but laugh. She'd never seen her friend so hopeless. "Bekah, have some faith in your brother! Or at least have some faith in *me*. No one is impossible to match. That's the beauty of this whole process. It's discovering what personality types and backgrounds work well together. Once your brother fills out the questionnaire I send him, and I have a chance to interview him, I'll have a better idea of who to introduce him to. Based on what you've already told me, I know what kind of woman *not* to pair him up with."

"You do? What kind?"

"Someone who's like him."

Bekah's mouth fell open. "But wouldn't someone like him understand him and get along well with him?"

"Sure. But there wouldn't be any tension to keep things interesting." A wide smile spread across her face. She didn't have a background in psychology, but she'd figured out long ago how people got along or didn't get along with each other. As the youngest in her family, she'd witnessed enough arguments and reconciliations to know how people ticked and also what ticked them off. "Being like-minded is good for most friendships and working relationships, but romantic ones need a bit of push and pull to keep the spark alive. Think about it, would you want to date someone exactly like you?"

Bekah pursed her lips as she thought. "I'm not sure. I've only gone out with a handful of guys and none of those relationships went anywhere. It's hard to date when you have two overprotective brothers watching out for you."

"I know all about that." She nodded sympathetically. "I have three overprotective sisters, not to mention an overeager mother who likes to get a little too involved in everyone's business. And they all wonder why I'm still single."

"Can't they just find someone for you from the client list? Since you guys already screen every person that signs up, they should be able to find someone they approve of."

Scarlett's brows shot up. "No way. My grandmother made that rule very clear from the beginning when she started the business. We're not allowed to date our clients."

"Not even if you're totally compatible?"

"Not even. We're not in this business to benefit ourselves. It's all about the client's needs. Anyway, I would rather meet a guy the old-fashioned way, like through a friend or at the store or on the street. I don't want to do it through a service. That's why I've avoided online dating completely. I just want it to be organic, you know?"

"I wish it were that easy to meet someone in person. It would make dating so much simpler."

"And so much more romantic. Just picture it—you see a man

from across a crowded room and make eye contact. Then the two of you strike up a conversation and find out all the things you have in common and all the things about him that are different but intriguing. There's no need to swipe left or right. The connection is just there."

She glanced around the restaurant as if the act could make her wishful thinking a reality. The effort was for naught when none of the male customers looked her way. It was to be expected when they were either dining with a female companion or eating alone, staring at their phone.

All except for one ...

Scarlett inhaled sharply the moment her eyes landed on a tall man walking across the restaurant. He looked to be in his mid-thirties with a short beard that covered an angular jawline. Professionally dressed in a white button-down shirt and black slacks, he strode over with a sense of purpose. The confident way he carried himself made her mouth go dry. When she didn't think he could be more attractive, he came close enough for her to see his features. Faint lines across his forehead made him appear distinguished. A prominent nose set off a pair of thin lips that curved up into a barely noticeable smile. And sparkling, electric blue eyes that swept up and down her face, making her stomach dip.

When he stopped at their table, Scarlett knew. This was the organic connection she'd hoped to find with a random stranger. She smiled up at him, ready to introduce herself, when Bekah noticed him.

"Hey, what are you doing here?"

The man reached into his pants pocket and pulled out a phone. "You forgot this at my office."

"I knew it! Thanks, Dev!"

Dev? No, it couldn't be ... Scarlett swallowed hard as she observed their exchange. Her worst fear was confirmed when Bekah looked over and announced, "Scarlett, meet my brother,

Devin. Dev, meet your new matchmaker, the incredible Scarlett Hayes."

That's when reality sunk like a boulder in Scarlett's stomach. The man she just fell for at first sight was totally and completely off-limits.

CHAPTER 3
Devin

She was the matchmaker who'd be finding him a wife?
Devin took another appraising glance at the woman his sister had dubbed "the incredible Scarlett Hayes." Incredible, huh? Judging from the lopsided bun on the top of her head and her wrinkle-free complexion, he wasn't holding his breath. She looked much too young and inexperienced to be in this line of business. Her ringless hand confirmed it, too. What could this woman know about finding a spouse when she herself was still single?

"It's so good to meet you, Mr. Kendall." Scarlett jumped up from her seat and offered her hand to him. "I've heard a lot about you from Bekah."

He grunted as her hand disappeared in his. Despite their slender appearance, her fingers gripped his with an impressive strength. At least her handshake meant business even if the rest of her didn't.

"Sit down, Dev." His sister pointed to the empty chair beside Scarlett's. "Have lunch with us."

He crossed his arms over his chest, ready to take his leave. Rushing over here had already put a kink in his busy schedule for the day. He'd made the effort though so Bekah wouldn't worry about where she'd misplaced her phone or be unable to reach him. With their brother away on tour again, he was the only one around for his sister when she needed help. "I'm good. You guys enjoy your meal. I need to head back to work."

"But what about lunch?"

"I've got mine in the microwave."

"It's cold by now. You might as well eat here. The food's a lot tastier than whatever is waiting for you at the office."

Devin hesitated. Food didn't matter much to him; as long as it curbed his appetite, he ate it. There were always other, far more pressing matters to spend time and effort on. But the dishes on the table did smell better than the same tray of indistinguishable grub he ate day after day. His mouth watered, tempting him to stay. The bright smile on Scarlett's face invited him as well. It offered him the same surprising warmth and openness that he'd seen in her photo.

He was both perturbed and intrigued at the same time.

How was it that she could be so friendly toward someone she'd just met? Or, perhaps, this was her show of good customer service? If so, it was at least a step in the right direction. He really ought to give her a chance to prove herself before he wrote her off. That was what his grandfather had done for him.

"If it helps, you can think of this as a working lunch," Scarlett suggested as she returned to her chair. "I'm sure you have questions about this whole matchmaking process. I can see the wheels turning in your head."

Devin blinked in surprise. Was he that easy to read or was she that good at figuring people out? "You're right. I do have questions."

"I'm sure Scarlett has all the answers!" Bekah exclaimed as she waved their server down for a menu. She passed it to Devin and motioned for him to take a look. "Order whatever you like, big bro. My treat!"

"Thanks," he uttered, trying hard not to roll his eyes. Bekah had received a sizeable inheritance from their grandfather, which she'd been spending much too quickly for his liking. The purse sitting on the chair beside hers looked new and expensive. He'd need to address her shopping habits with her again, but that would have to wait for another time.

He sat down next to Scarlett and quickly perused the menu. Once he'd placed his order with the server, he found himself at the center of attention. Two pairs of eyes, one blue like his and the other a vibrant green, stared back at him.

"What questions do you have for me?" Scarlett asked. There was that smile of hers again, shining bright like a lighthouse. He wondered how much coffee was responsible for it. Or was she naturally this peppy? "I'm happy to answer whatever you ask. Nothing's off the table."

"Nothing, you say?"

"Nothing. I understand how daunting this whole process can be, especially if you haven't dated much before."

He quirked a brow at her response. "What gives you the impression I haven't dated much?"

"Bekah mentioned it."

"She did, did she?" He eyed his sister, whose mouth was conveniently too full to answer.

"It's nothing to be embarrassed about," Scarlett continued, her tone full of sympathy. "I know a man as busy as you doesn't have much time to date. But don't you worry, that's what I'm here for. I'll have you back in the saddle before you know it."

He wasn't sure what tales his sister had told Scarlett about him, but he didn't appreciate being pitied. The concern in her voice made him feel like a pet project of hers. Like some kind of stray animal that she'd found on the side of the road and brought home to rehabilitate. The thought left a bad taste in his mouth. He grabbed the glass of water their server had brought and chugged it down.

Everything about this arrangement was wrong. If it weren't for his grandfather's will, he would never even consider enlisting the help of a matchmaker. Devin couldn't believe he'd succumbed to this level of desperation. But there was one thing he needed to make clear to Scarlett. "For the record, I'm neither embarrassed nor helpless. I am short on time, though, so I hope you know what you're doing. If you don't mind me asking, how much experience do you have and how many couples have you successfully matched?"

Her cheeks pinkened and she sat up straighter in her chair. The bun on her head swayed back and forth with the effort, but her expression remained unfazed. "I have one word for both of your questions and that word is *enough*. It's not always about quantity, Mr. Kendall. In my line of work, quality is what matters."

Devin smirked. She thought fast on her feet; he had to give her that. Scarlett had what his grandfather would have called gumption. Even with her lack of experience, he'd be willing to give her a chance based on her wit alone. A fiery spark lit up her eyes as she held his gaze, unblinking.

He was so caught up in their unspoken staring game, he didn't notice that the server had dropped off his dish until he smelled the aroma of garlic butter. Hunger won out, and he turned his focus to his plate of sirloin steak with pasta. In between bites, he remarked, "I like your confidence. I look forward to seeing you bring your A game."

"I will. I promise to do my all to help you find your perfectly imperfect match."

"What do you mean by that, Scarlett?" Bekah asked. "Don't you want to find Devin a perfect match?"

Devin nodded. His sister had spoken his thoughts out loud. "It sounds like you're giving yourself an easy out before you even start. Are you or are you not going to find me the perfect match?"

"Of course, I am," Scarlett reassured them. "But let me

explain. The fact of the matter is that it's impossible to find anyone a perfect match. They don't exist. No person that ever walked this earth is perfect, except for Jesus. Everyone has faults and hang-ups and imperfections. Even you, Mr. Kendall."

He stopped chewing long enough to glance at her out of the corner of his eye. Was he imagining things, or did she sound particularly giddy when she'd said that last line? He swallowed his bite of steak before turning toward her. "Are you this blunt with all your clients?"

"If by blunt you mean honest, then yes, I am. I give realistic expectations when it comes to dating. I'm here to set you up for success."

"So, what you're saying—"

"Um, Dev," Bekah suddenly interrupted him, "you've got something—"

He held up a finger to stop her. "One sec, sis. What you're saying," he directed his question to Scarlett again, "is that successful dating requires me to lower my standards when it comes to women?"

"Not your standards, your expectations."

His grip tightened around his fork as her bright green eyes blinked at him all too innocently. "What's the difference?"

"How should I put it?" She cocked her head to the side, her brows furrowed. "Well, for example, you may have a certain standard for how well-groomed and clean you want to appear, but you also need to have realistic expectations that sometimes things don't go as planned. For instance ... when you're eating, and you end up with sauce on your face."

Bekah broke out into uncontrollable laughter. "Oh, that's a good one, Scarlett!"

She shrugged sheepishly. "I couldn't help myself. It's kind of the perfect analogy."

Devin froze in place as his eyes darted back and forth from one side of the table to the other. It took him a good three seconds to process the knowing looks on the two women's faces before he caught on to their inside joke. "I don't appreciate being the butt of someone's joke."

"I tried to tell you, Dev, but you didn't let me finish." Bekah winced. "And for the record, I wasn't laughing *at* you."

"You were laughing with me then? News flash, I wasn't laughing." He grabbed his cloth napkin from off his lap and wiped the corners of his mouth. He had half a mind to get up and leave. He didn't need to be here, and he certainly didn't need to be humiliated. He pushed back his chair and stood up.

"Mr. Kendall, please stay," Scarlett pled, placing her hand on his arm. "I didn't mean to make you feel uncomfortable. My Nanna always used to say I needed more tact. I should've thought it through before I opened my mouth. I apologize. I'm on your side, I promise."

He released a heavy breath and unclenched his fists. There was something about her words that reined in his emotions. She sounded genuinely sorry. If she could be willing to extend an olive branch, he would accept it. He gave her a curt nod and sat back down.

Scarlett suddenly leaned forward, her nose mere inches from his. Her eyes narrowed in on his mouth, catching him off guard. Before he knew what was happening, she reached over and swiped her thumb across his chin. "You had some sauce on your beard, but you're good now."

She then returned to talking to Bekah, leaving him too dazed to speak. That's when Devin realized his sister was right. Scarlett Hayes *was* incredible, in the most surprising and confusing way. She was unlike any woman he'd ever met, and he didn't know what to make of that.

CHAPTER 4
Scarlett

Thank You, Lord, for good sense.

This was Scarlett's prayer Tuesday morning when she arrived at the office ready to tackle the day. In between her morning devotions and her drive over, she'd had plenty of time to reflect on yesterday's lunch. Especially on all the red flags that she'd spotted when it came to Bekah's brother.

Red flag number one: his big, fragile ego.

Red flag number two: his stick-in-the-mud personality.

Red flag number three: his jaded outlook on life.

She pitied the woman who'd end up with Mr. Kendall. He was about as pleasant as a root canal. It would take someone strong, sweet, and Christlike to love him.

Thankfully, that wouldn't be her.

She might have been attracted to his charisma and good looks when he walked into the restaurant, but as soon as he'd opened his mouth, she'd gotten a taste of reality. One that was bitter and painful to swallow. No amount of sugar in the world would be able to sweeten that man up. He was like a big, black storm cloud filled with enough rain to douse anyone's good mood. Even if she could date Devin, she'd lost all interest in him. Her only desire now was to get him matched, and matched quickly. The less time she had to spend with him, the better.

"Red!" a bubbly voice called out to her from the office doorway. "Mom said you signed on a client! How'd you find one so fast?"

Scarlett glanced up from her computer monitor to see her third-oldest sister, Emerald, bound into the room. With her long, red locks, creamy complexion, and hourglass figure, she was often called the prettiest Hayes sister. She made heads turn, not only with her beauty but also with her sociable personality. Though they were four years apart, Scarlett felt the closest to her. "It wasn't me. He just kind of fell into my lap. I'm friends with his sister and she introduced us. She did me a huge favor, but I've got my work cut out for me. This guy is not going to be easy to match."

Emerald sat down in the chair on the other side of the small desk. Her brows wiggled up and down as she leaned forward. "This has drama written all over it. Do tell. I want all the juicy details."

"He's a CEO, mid-thirties, type A personality, and a workaholic. Very uptight and critical. And he had the gall to question my credentials!" An involuntary shudder ran through her body as she recalled his haughty tone. "I nearly lost my cool with him. The only way I managed to keep it together was to remind myself that I could be the bigger person. But I totally had to repent afterwards for all the mean names I called him in my head."

"Wow. He sounds like a piece of work." Her lips curved into a small smile. "But you know what Nanna used to say: Hard times bring us closer to the Lord. I have a feeling you're going to be praying a lot more, thanks to this client."

Scarlett groaned. That was not what she wanted to hear. "Why can't we grow closer to God without going through hard times? Isn't there another way?"

"I'm afraid not. But if you find one, let me know. In the meantime, you're going to have to learn how to get along with Mr.

Drama King. Especially if you want to keep both of your eyebrows. You know how competitive Amber and Capri are," she added, referring to their older sisters. "I bet they're cold-calling all the single execs they can find at Facebook and Google."

"I wouldn't be surprised." Her sisters were all gifted in ways she wasn't. Amber was a literal genius with multiple patents to her name. Capri had been a competitive swimmer during college and had qualified for the Olympics. Emerald had been winning beauty pageants since she was a kid. Being at the top was in their blood. Scarlett couldn't follow in their footsteps even if she tried. But at least she was one step ahead of them for once in her life. "What about you, Em? Do you have any prospects?"

"I'm interviewing one this morning. She's a CEO at a start-up, but she seems to have a good work-life balance. She's super sweet and ready to settle down." She tapped a red fingernail against her lower lip. "You know what I'm thinking?"

Scarlett caught on to the sparkle in her sister's blue eyes. "You want to see if your client is a good fit for my client?"

"Bingo! Let's touch base later today and go over their profiles together."

"Sounds good."

"Cool. I gotta run, but I'll catch you later, Red."

With a quick wave, Emerald shut the door behind her as she left. Scarlett twisted in her seat as she looked around her office. The simple, white decor that her mother had insisted on for all the individual offices contrasted greatly with her bright pink suit. It was one of those days when she'd started out wearing neutral hues but had changed to something with a pop of color. She'd needed a shift in her perspective to jumpstart her mood. That and a large mug of chai tea latte and her favorite lemon scone. She needed all the help she could get to find her client a match.

Their company database housed a couple hundred profiles of male and female clients from throughout the Bay Area. Not surprisingly, there were more of the former, men in their late thirties to early fifties who had been too invested in their work to date. Each person had to fill out a five-page questionnaire when they started, then go through an in-depth interview before being matched. Bekah's brother had sent her his answers early this morning. Scarlett had about an hour to review them before they were scheduled to meet in person.

She pulled up his form on the computer and began skimming the first page. Her eyes widened as she scrolled through the questions addressing different areas of his life and his preferences. Pithy one-liners filled each section.

For lifestyle, he'd written *busy*.

Under family values, he'd answered *strong*.

And for communication style, he'd said *clear*.

The details she needed were nowhere to be found. Did he expect her to read his mind?

Too impatient to wait for their appointed time, she grabbed her phone and dialed his cell phone number.

A gruff, masculine voice answered after the fourth ring. "Hello?"

"Mr. Kendall, this is Scarlett Hayes."

"Who?"

"Scarlett Hayes, your matchmaker, Bekah's friend. We met yesterday at lunch."

"Right, Ms. Hayes. Isn't our meeting scheduled for later this morning?"

"Yes, I know we're on for nine thirty, but I'm calling you now because I just reviewed the questionnaire you sent back to me, and I noticed a lot of spaces were left blank."

"And?"

"And that doesn't give me much to work with. If I'm to find you an appropriate match, I need to understand you better. I need more information."

"How much more information?"

"It doesn't have to be an essay, but I would appreciate at least half a page for each question. That's how much my other clients have written."

"Here's the thing—I'm not like your other clients. My schedule is packed from morning till night. That's why I signed up for your services in the first place: because I don't have time to date, much less fill out a five-page questionnaire."

"I understand you're busy, but—"

"How many CEOs have you worked with, Ms. Hayes?"

There he was questioning her expertise again. She rubbed her temples, feeling a headache coming on. Why was he being so difficult? Her sister was right when she'd called Devin Kendall a drama king. It was quite appropriate how his initials were D.K. as well. She inhaled deeply and prayed for patience. "Why does it matter? I've had plenty of experience working with people in all types of careers."

"The difference is that I have a company to run and thousands of employees under my care. I cannot afford to spend my time on trivial matters."

"Trivial matters? I don't think you're understanding the gravity of the situation, Mr. Kendall. We're not talking about finding you your next car or house. I'm helping you to find a spouse, a lifelong partner! Unless you don't intend to stay married for the rest of your life?"

He balked. "Of course, I intend to stay married. Marriage is not something I take lightly, Ms. Hayes."

"Then it would be to your benefit to put a little more effort into this process. I want the best for you, Mr. Kendall, but you need to want that for yourself, too."

Silence fell on the line for a good five seconds before he spoke again. "I see your point."

Scarlett beamed. There was some common sense in that thick skull of his after all. Now that he was willing to admit she was right, they could do some actual work. "I'm glad you agree. Now, I know you're a busy man, so if there's any way I can make this easier for you, just let me know."

"Other than requesting that the questionnaire be cut in half?" he asked drolly.

She let out a surprised chuckle. "You have a sense of humor!"

"It's known to make an appearance now and then."

"Well, I'm glad to see this side of you. Women love men who can make them laugh. I will definitely highlight this in your profile, Mr. Kendall."

"Good. Feel free to call me Devin."

"All right, Devin. You may feel free to call me Scarlett. Or Red. That's what my family calls me."

"Do you let all your clients call you Red?"

"No, but Bekah's like a sister to me, so I suppose that makes you like family. I figure we'll be spending a lot of time together throughout this process, so I want our relationship to be friendly and fun."

"Yet professional? That's an oxymoron if I've ever heard one."

"Not at all. It's possible to be professional *and* have fun. Stick with me and I'll show you how."

"I'll believe it when I see it. I'd like to see you find a way to make that questionnaire enjoyable."

Scarlett straightened in her chair. "Challenge accepted," she declared in a firm tone. "Just to let you know, I never back down from a challenge. I'll find a way to make answering those questions fun *and* efficient. It'll be the CEO-friendly version, perfect for busy VIPs like you."

"And what happens if you don't succeed?"

Her mind was already spinning a mile a minute with ideas. She couldn't afford to consider the possibility of losing, not when her reputation was on the line. "That won't happen."

"Is that so?" He snickered. "I would be more careful if I were you. You've heard the saying 'pride comes before a fall'?"

"Yes, but this isn't my pride speaking. It's confidence." She glanced at her watch, eager to end the call. "I'll see you at my office in forty-eight minutes, Devin. Be prepared to have fun!"

Scarlett hung up, feeling quite pleased with herself. She knew exactly what to do and whom to ask for help. A moment later, she had her friend on the line.

"Bekah, I need you to tell me everything you know about your brother ..."

CHAPTER 5
Devin

Devin had no idea what to expect when he showed up at Scarlett's work, but a welcoming committee was not it. As soon as he stepped through the front door, three animated women approached him.

The redhead greeted him with a blindingly white smile. "Hello there! I'm Emerald. How may I help you? Are you interested in finding your perfect match?"

"I can assist you!" the taller brunette exclaimed as she gave him a quick once-over. "A man of your stature needs someone more experienced. I'm Capri, by the way."

The shortest of the three stepped forward and extended her hand. "Welcome to Party of Two. I'm Amber Hayes, one of the owners of our prestigious award-winning company. What brings you here today, Mister ..."

"Kendall. Devin Kendall." He glanced around the small waiting room with its modern-looking furniture. Its purple and gold color scheme was much brighter and playful than the sterile white of his workplace, but it matched what he knew of Scarlett so far. Her personality was equal parts bright and eager. He wondered if these three women were related to her. Judging by their similar facial features, he presumed they were sisters. "I'm here to see Scarlett. We have a nine-thirty appointment."

Emerald gasped. "*You're* Scarlett's client? Oh, she wasn't kidding!"

He quirked a brow in her direction. "What do you mean by that?"

"It's nothing! Forget I said anything."

"I happen to have a very good memory, so please don't insult me."

Her face flushed. "I wouldn't dream of it, Mr. Kendall. It really was nothing."

Amber shot Emerald a wide-eyed look that told Devin she was the oldest sibling. "Emerald, how many times do I need to remind you that the client is always right? Tell Mr. Kendall what Scarlett said. She wasn't kidding about what?"

"Just about how, um, tall and handsome he is."

Devin's jaw hung slack as he processed this information. Was Scarlett attracted to him? "She said that?"

"She also mentioned how hardworking and successful you are," Emerald rushed on to add. "Enough talking! Let me take you to her office. Right this way!"

He followed her down a short hallway to the last door on the right. There was no time to consider the ramifications of Emerald's revelation, but he did wonder if that was why Scarlett had been so touchy with him yesterday. His jaw clenched with frustration. Women! Who knew how their minds worked? Even if he cared to understand them, it was nearly impossible to do so. All he knew was that he ought to keep his distance from his matchmaker. The last thing he wanted to do was give her any wrong ideas.

"Red?" Emerald called out and gave the door a quick knock. "Your client, Mr. Kendall, is here."

"Coming!" The impossibly cheerful voice grew louder as the door swung open. "Hi, Devin!"

Devin blinked hard as if a bright ray of light had blinded him.

He found himself face to face with a woman dressed in professional attire. She wore a bright pink pantsuit with a gray sweater and matching pink heels. Long, dark curls drew attention to her creamy complexion. Her light makeup had a natural appeal. But it was her smile—bright, sweet, and welcoming—that paralyzed his tongue. For the first time in his adult life, he felt his neck flush. This woman, whoever she was, could not be more beautiful.

"Have a seat! I don't expect you to stand for our meeting."

Hearing Scarlett's voice coming from her mouth made him do a double take. How could it be? The person he'd met yesterday had been a shadow of a woman—young, inexperienced, and too confident for her own good. The woman standing before him today appeared polished, put together, and mature.

Dumbfounded, he sat down in the chair Scarlett directed him to. By this time, her sister had left the office, leaving the two of them alone. Devin swallowed hard and wiped his palms along his black slacks. He needed to get his head back in the game. There was only one reason he was here and that was to save his family's company. He couldn't afford to be distracted, especially not by something as shallow as appearances. Running a hand down his face, he took a deep breath and strengthened his resolve. He could stay focused. He *had* to stay focused.

"I'm so glad you could take time out of your busy schedule to meet in person, Devin." Scarlett pushed a piece of paper across the desk to him. "I promised a fun and efficient interview, so here it is. I'll be taking notes, so you can sit back and relax."

Relax? Easier said than done. His senses were on heightened alert with Scarlett only two feet away. The sweet floral scent of her perfume hung in the air, muddling his thoughts. Crossing his legs, he rested an ankle over his knee, then squared his jaw. "I'll relax when this is over. I have no time to waste, Ms. Hayes. Let's get started."

"Oh-kay," she muttered under her breath, "someone woke up on the wrong side of the universe today."

He shot her an indignant look. "Excuse me?"

"I think I have the answer to my first question. Let me guess, you're a night owl?"

He glanced down at the paper that had two columns of words listed. The first comparison was "Morning bird or Night owl." Smirking, he remarked, "This is how you're conducting the questionnaire, by doing one of those social media challenges?"

"You're familiar with 'This or That'? I didn't take you for an Instagram kind of guy."

"I'm not. I only follow my sister's and brother's accounts. Bekah's had some 'This or That' posts, but none like this that I recall."

"That's because I made this one myself," she declared proudly. "Now, was I right in guessing that you're not a morning person?"

"That's right."

"Yes!" She made a note on her paper. "What about the next one? Do you like receiving gifts or spending quality time together? Hold on, let me guess first!"

He almost rolled his eyes at her enthusiastic tone. This *was* the same woman he'd met yesterday, after all. Despite her professional dress, she still had the same childlike spirit. This realization gave him some relief. There was no possibility that he'd be attracted to someone as young and green as Scarlett. But he did find her enthusiasm somewhat appealing. "Go on," he humored her, "take a wild guess."

"I think you like gifts more. You don't strike me as a people person."

He sneered, not appreciating the way she wrinkled her nose. "I'm not paying you to insult me."

"It's not an insult at all. I'm speaking the truth, which is what you're paying me to do. Trust me, you don't want me to lie and flatter you. That wouldn't be of any benefit to you or to this process." Her tone turned serious. "Everything I'm doing is to help you. People who are self-aware have an easier time in their relationships."

Why did every meeting with Scarlett seem like a therapy session? She somehow always found a way to turn the tables and make him feel like he was the problem and that he was the one who needed to change. But what about her?

"Isn't it your job to find me a woman I'm compatible with? If you do your job right, I should have no problem getting along with her." *Definitely a lot better than you and I get along,* he thought to himself. If he'd learned anything from Scarlett so far, it was the type of woman to *avoid*, namely someone like her. He could do without her smart-alecky attitude and incessant comebacks.

"I don't know what world you've been living in, Devin, but every relationship on earth, whether it's with family members or friends or colleagues, requires work. We're all sinners and works in progress. Nobody's perfect, not even you."

"So you've told me before." His foot shook in annoyance. What was it with this woman? For someone who supposedly thought he was handsome, she didn't seem so enamored with him. Was this her way of playing it cool and being intentional about setting professional boundaries? Why was she so difficult to understand?

He narrowed his eyes and locked gazes with Scarlett across the desk. Her expression softened the longer they stared. After about five seconds, she looked away and cleared her throat.

"How about we try the next activity?" she suggested. "You might like it more. It's called Truth or Lie. You list twelve things about yourself, but make half of them lies, and I'll try to guess which ones those are."

He took the pen she handed him. "I can write anything I want?"

"Anything you want."

Devin glanced down at the blank spaces on the paper,

wondering where to begin. It wasn't often that he needed to make up lies about himself. This would require some brainstorming, especially if he wanted to win.

Scarlett was right. He *would* enjoy this more.

For the next ten minutes, he jotted down his twelve facts. When he was done, he slid the paper back to Scarlett's side.

She read it in complete silence. It was a good minute before she looked up. "This is good, Devin. I'm impressed at how hard you made it for me."

He couldn't stop the corners of his mouth from curving up. "I mean business. Go ahead and make your guesses."

"Okay. I think these are the lies—you went bungee jumping on your eighteenth birthday, you go to the gym every other day, you love mushrooms, you wanted to be a zookeeper when you were young, you don't know how to ice skate, and you were in a band when you were in college. Am I right?"

"Close." He couldn't resist grinning at the shock on her face. "One out of six isn't bad."

"No, what?! Only one of them is a lie and the rest are true? How can that be?" Shaking her head in disbelief, she studied the paper again. "You *do* know how to ice skate?"

"Wrong. I've never ice skated in my life."

"Never? You never went when you were a kid?"

"Never." His childhood had been spent keeping the house in order and his siblings fed while his dad worked day and night. There had been little time for playing. He gave a quick shake of his head, not willing to divulge more. "I didn't have any interest in going."

"You should give it a try sometime! You never know, you might be a natural on the ice."

"I don't have the time."

"That's just an excuse. You can always make time."

"I would if that was something I wanted to do, but I don't."

She nodded. "Okay, that's fair."

He expected her to interject a *but,* however, there was only silence. "You're letting me win this one?"

"This isn't a competition, Devin. We're on the same team."

"So you like to remind me."

Her long lashes fluttered as she grinned. "You sound like you don't believe me."

"I just find you to be—how shall I put it—quite spirited in your responses to me. You seem to enjoy putting me in my place."

Her nose wrinkled. "I won't lie. I do enjoy seeing you squirm. Is that bad?"

Bad? It was only bad if Devin acknowledged how much his body warmed at the sight of Scarlett's smile. He was growing fond of the mischievous sparkle in her eyes. How had she gotten under his skin so quickly?

As much as he hated to admit it, Devin didn't mind bantering back and forth like this. It was a nice break from his work, which he hadn't thought about once since he'd arrived. There was something about Scarlett that made it easy to let his guard down and loosen up. When she wasn't saying things that made his eyes roll, she made him want to smile, or smirk at the very least. He found himself enjoying their conversation and even possibly her company.

"Maybe I should be nicer," she continued as she waved the piece of paper in her hands, "at least until you tell me which ones of these are true."

"Or maybe"—he shrugged innocently—"I'll never tell you, so you'll have to continue being nice to me."

CHAPTER 6
Scarlett

Scarlett burst out with a laugh. "Look at you! You do have a fun side after all, Devin Kendall. I can't wait to discover more of it."

Devin Kendall had a sense of humor—who would have thought? Certainly not her when they had started their meeting. But the activities that she'd prepared had proven to be a success. Not only was he sharing about himself, but he was smiling, too.

Scarlett said a prayer of thanks. This was turning out to be better than she'd expected. Now she just needed to keep him talking because she really wanted to know more about him. He was certainly a complicated individual, which could make her job of matching him difficult.

Emerald had been right. She'd need God's help with this client in more ways than one.

"So, if the not knowing how to ice skate is true," Scarlett began, "then it must be the mushrooms! The truth is that you hate mushrooms, am I right?"

He shook his head. "Wrong. I like fungi."

"Ha!" She threw her head back as a wave of laughter rolled

through her. "Sorry, that word always makes me laugh for some reason."

One of his brows arched. "You find fungi funny?"

Scarlett bit her lower lip and tried her best to remain professional. The effort worked for barely two seconds when a chuckle flew from her mouth. "Please stop! If you're trying to distract me, it's working, but I'd like for us to focus on getting through this interview."

"As you wish."

She wiped the corners of her eyes as she caught her breath. "Don't tell me you're a fan of *The Princess Bride*?"

"Come again?"

"The movie *The Princess Bride*. 'As you wish' is a well-known line that the male lead, Westley, says to Buttercup, the female lead. You've never seen it?"

That same raised eyebrow of his twitched. "Do I look like someone who would watch a movie with a character named Buttercup?"

"Well, you also don't look like someone who would go bungee jumping."

"But I did."

Her jaw dropped. She couldn't process how someone as tightly wound as Devin would subject himself to such a wild activity. "I'm in shock right now."

"I jumped from a bridge about a hundred feet off the ground."

"That's amazing! I'm deathly afraid of heights. Just riding in a glass elevator makes my palms sweat. Who in the world was able to convince you to jump off a bridge?"

"My brother Jace. Ever since he saw James Bond jump off a dam in *GoldenEye*, he wanted to try it himself. He found a place up near Sacramento and talked me into going the summer after high school graduation. He said if I went with him, he'd never ask me for another favor as long as he lived."

"You couldn't have believed that he'd keep that promise."

"Of course not. But it was worth it to see him happy."

Scarlett couldn't help but smile. Devin had a heart after all. The more she learned about him, the more impressed she was. "You're a good brother."

He dismissed her compliment with a wave of his hand. "Jace had a hard time when he was growing up. I do what I can to be there for him."

"That says a lot about you, Devin. Women love a man who takes care of his family." She couldn't be sure, but she thought she saw a slight blush color his cheeks before he tipped his head down. For someone so sure of himself, she was surprised he had a hard time taking a compliment. Not wanting to make him more uncomfortable, she returned to her guessing. "Okay, I'm sure this next one is a lie. You claim to have been in a band during college. Unless it was a band made up of business majors ..."

He lifted his gaze and met hers. The smirk she'd grown used to seeing on his face reappeared. "You think you have me all figured out, don't you? You assume business majors can't sing or play instruments?"

"I didn't say that. But being in a band presumes that you're someone who likes being in front of an audience and performing and, correct me if I'm wrong, I really don't think that's who you are."

"Fine, you're right."

"Yes!" Scarlett tapped her heels under her desk in a little victory dance. "I knew it. You weren't in a band."

He cleared his throat. "No, you're still wrong. I *was* in a band, but I left because I didn't like performing on stage. That part you guessed right."

Scarlett nearly swallowed her tongue. He might as well have said that he'd been part of the circus because that would've been just as unbelievable. "What instrument did you play and what type of band was it?"

"Guitar and keyboard. Mostly pop songs. Jace wrote the lyrics, and I came up with the melodies. He recruited two guys from our Economics class to play the bass and drums. They still tour with him to this day."

She threw up her hands and tossed aside the paper she'd been holding. "You're telling me you could've been a rock star like your brother, but you gave it up to work in the corporate world? Why would you do that?"

"Besides not wanting to be in the spotlight?" he drawled in that no-nonsense way that she was becoming familiar with. His tone was more matter of fact than snarky. "Our grandfather needed someone to help with the family business. Jace and Bekah weren't interested, and none of our cousins were either, so it was left to me."

"You did it out of duty."

His expression grew thoughtful. "In a way, yes. It was also a gesture of appreciation to my grandfather. He took the three of us in after our mom got sick."

"What about your dad? Where was he?"

"He took off one day and didn't come back. Haven't heard from him since."

Scarlett's heart plummeted to her feet. The faraway look in his eyes revealed a lot more than he said. Bekah had mentioned their family's history to her before, but she'd said she had been too young to remember most of it. Devin, on the other hand, sounded like he remembered far too much. "That's awful. I'm so sorry you went through all of that."

"Don't be. We were better off with my grandfather." A muscle in his jaw clenched as he ran a hand through his hair. "That's enough of my past. You can leave those details out of my profile. I doubt any woman would find that appealing."

"Oh, but that's where you're wrong. Women love guys with a tragic past. Haven't you seen *Beauty and the Beast*? Never mind, you don't look like the type of guy who watches animated films."

"As much as I hate to admit it, I have, at least three times. It was Bekah's favorite."

"Then you should be able to understand why Belle fell for the Beast the more she got to know him."

"Because she liked rehabilitating wild animals?"

"No, silly! Because she saw past the Beast's gruff exterior and into his heart. And she knew there was a genuinely sweet guy inside who just needed to be loved. And since women tend to be caretakers, they find that challenge kind of appealing."

That muscle in his jaw twitched again. "And you think I'm like the Beast? That the love of a woman will heal all my scars?"

She took a moment to reply, weighing her words carefully. "I don't know. I don't know you well enough yet, but from what I do know so far, I think you have a soft side that you keep tucked away. A woman's love won't heal you completely—only God's love can do that—but it could help."

His expression hardened. "I'm not here for anyone's pity. If you intend to match me with one of those caretaker types, I'll pass."

The growly man from yesterday had reappeared. Scarlett softened her tone as she replied, "Noted. Tell me then, what are you looking for in a wife?"

Without hesitation, he replied, "Someone who thinks for herself and speaks her mind. I want her to have her own interests and goals. She needs to be able to stand on her own two feet."

Scarlett quirked a brow. She appreciated that he had respect for strong, independent women, but she wondered if he realized what he was asking for. "Have you ever dated a woman like that?"

"Why does it matter if I have or not?"

"It matters because this hypothetical woman that you're talking about sounds a lot like you. And from what I've observed in my line of work, having two people with the same intense and passionate personality traits together can get quite explosive. Kaboom!" She imitated the sound of an explosion. "It would be like being married to yourself. Can you imagine what that'd be like?"

"You make it sound like a bad thing." He tapped his fingers on his knee, his irritation on full display. "Are you implying that I'm hard to get along with?"

"No, not you, specifically. But think about it. When you have two individuals who both speak their minds all the time, who's going to listen? You need balance in a relationship. You'd be better off with a woman who's softer around the edges. Trust me on this, Devin. I've been matching couples for a while now. I know what combination works."

"If you know what works so well, why don't I see a ring on *your* finger?"

A flash of heat raced up Scarlett's neck and settled in her cheeks. A mixture of disdain and embarrassment tightened her chest and made it hard to breathe. It took every ounce of resolve in her heart to not tear up. She hadn't cried over her ex since they broke up five years ago; why was she on the verge of crying now? Probably because Devin was a master at pushing her buttons and he'd just zeroed in on her most sensitive one. No matter. God loved and accepted her—fractured heart and all—and she didn't need any man's approval to feel okay about herself.

She raised her chin with as much confidence as she could muster. "If you must know, I was engaged once."

"What happened, if you don't mind me asking?"

His surprisingly gentle tone made it easier to look him in the eye. "Long story short, his family didn't think I was good enough for them. They're all involved in politics, and I didn't fit the mold of what they wanted in a daughter-in-law."

"That's harsh. Did your ex think the same way?"

"Not at first. He wasn't like the rest of his family when we met in college, but things changed after graduation. His parents got him working on a campaign for a local senator. That's when he started thinking more about money, prestige, and power. Before that, we'd had an entirely different future planned out. We were going to get married, and he'd become a legal aid lawyer to help the disadvantaged. I was going to stay home with the kids, and we'd be the perfect middle-class American family," she added with a bittersweet smile.

"With your 2.5 kids, living in a house with a white picket fence?"

Scarlett rolled her eyes at his light, teasing tone. "Yes. And a dog. You forgot to mention the dog."

"Ah, yes, Fido. My apologies to the sweet beast."

His deadpan delivery had her cracking a smile. "Well, it's obvious now what your lie was. You don't like animals. So, you must not have wanted to be a zookeeper when you were young."

"That was actually true. I wanted to work at the zoo until I realized at age ten how smelly the animals can be. But I still have membership and make it a point to go at least once a year."

Scarlett blinked. She sure had read him wrong. If that was the case... "Then your lie is that you go to the gym?"

"Correct."

She gave him a thorough once-over, her gaze traveling from his broad shoulders to his toned chest that stretched the material of his shirt, and down to his strong, masculine hands. Every inch of him was toned and fit. She knew some people had good genes, but there was no way he woke up like this. If the silence stretching between them hadn't been verging on awkward, she might have stared longer. Instead, she forced her gaze up to his equally attractive face. "You could've fooled me. How did you get all your muscles then?"

"I didn't say I don't go to the gym at all. I go every day, not every other day—that part was the lie."

"Oh! Well, that totally makes more sense. Of course, you'd need to go every day to look that hot—" She clamped her mouth shut. There were no words to express the extent of her mortification. "Pretend you didn't hear that."

"I didn't hear anything," he quipped, "but I appreciate the compliment."

Scarlett gulped, her cheeks flaming hot. So much for being professional and in control. She needed to stay alert around this man before she got herself in any more trouble.

"I think I have all the information I need from you. Thanks again for coming in today." She rose to her feet, giving Devin a hint that their meeting was over. When he didn't budge, she clarified: "I'm sure you have a very busy schedule. You're free to go now, Mr. Kendall."

"That's too bad. I was just starting to have fun." His tone reflected the mischievous sparkle in his eyes. He stood up and headed for the door, then paused when he got there. "Come to think of it, Ms. Hayes, you're someone who speaks her mind. You're not exactly the type of woman I'm looking for, but you're not far from it, and we get along well. I rest my case."

Scarlett burst out with a laugh. "You can't be serious. We hardly agree on anything. We're like oil and water, or more like oil and fire."

He narrowed his gaze at her and smirked. "As long as we stay away from water, we'll be fine. Good day, Ms. Hayes."

Good day, her foot. What kind of logic was that? The only positive thing Scarlett could think of as she rolled her eyes was, *At least the man has impeccable taste.*

CHAPTER 7
Devin

Devin had discovered something he liked about Scarlett—seeing her squirm. He couldn't stop replaying the scene from her office a few days ago when he'd called her out for ogling him.

Even now as he drove home from work, he could picture her wide eyes and red cheeks. The best part was that he hadn't even been trying to goad her; she'd slipped up on her own. And what a good gaffe it'd been. After that, Scarlett had only offered him a small, polite smile when they parted ways. Devin didn't mind the change in attitude. If it helped speed up this matchmaking process, it would be a benefit to them both. She'd win that ridiculous contest with her sisters, and he'd ensure the family business stayed in the right hands.

If only he could settle on a woman to go out with.

The dozen profiles that Scarlett sent him yesterday still sat in his inbox, waiting. He'd gone through each of the portfolios and photos twice, but he still wasn't sure which ones to pick. All of them had attended Ivy League schools and held impressive positions. Vice Presidents, attorneys, surgeons—there was even a CEO in the mix. The caliber of their resumes far outweighed his. Scarlett had exceeded his expectations in presenting him with such worthy candidates. She had delivered what he'd asked for—strong, independent, and successful women. Women exactly the opposite of his late mother.

That had been his mother's one fault. A fault that led to her sacrificing her own health and well-being for her family and ultimately resulted in her demise.

Sighing, Devin reined in his emotions and focused on the road. He drove through a small, gated community in Los Gatos where he and his siblings lived. They had inherited their grandfather's two-story, five-bedroom house, the one they had grown up in and he and Jace had moved out of when they'd graduated high school. Bekah had never left, choosing instead to stay with their grandfather and enjoy the benefit of a full-time staff who cooked and cleaned for them.

Devin had only returned recently after Bekah complained about the house being too quiet. With Jace gone on tour half the year, he was the only family around for their sister to rely on. He made it a point to go home early enough to eat dinner with Bekah a couple of times a week. This meant he'd have to finish up his work at home, even on a Friday like today, but it was worth it to see her smile.

It was this bright smile that greeted him from the dining table when he walked through the door moments later.

"Hey, Dev! Guess what we're having for dinner? Chicken pot pie!" Bekah exclaimed as he took a seat across from her. "Too bad Jace isn't here to enjoy it."

He shrugged off his jacket and loosened his tie. "I'm sure he's getting plenty of good meals on the road. There's no need to feel sorry for him."

"I know, but it's not the same as eating a homecooked meal with your family." She dished some of the pot pie onto his plate, along with a serving of salad. "Did your meeting run late? I thought you'd be home earlier."

He took the linen napkin beside his gold-rimmed plate and placed it on his lap. "Sorry about the wait. These board members aren't the easiest people to deal with."

Her brows drew together as she frowned. "Sorry to hear that. I bet they're still getting used to working with you instead of Grandad. Your personalities are pretty different."

"You can say that again," he scoffed as he picked up his fork. Their grandfather had been as sociable as Devin was reserved. He'd had a talent for connecting with people, one Devin had unfortunately not inherited. That's why it usually took hours for him and the board to come to an agreement about any matter, big or small. He should have told Bekah to start dinner without him. "Next time just eat first."

"I don't mind waiting. I'd rather wait than eat alone." Wrinkling her nose, she exclaimed, "Dev, we didn't say grace yet!"

"Right." He set down his fork and bowed his head. "Why don't you do the honors?"

Bekah prayed, "Lord, we thank You for this abundance of food. And we ask that You watch over Jace and keep him safe while he's away. And please provide a good wife for Devin, someone who will know how to support him. In Jesus' name, amen."

Devin held back the smirk twitching the corners of his mouth. This was the first time Bekah had prayed for him about this topic. He appreciated the intent behind her words, but he certainly didn't agree with it. "Why do you think I need a woman to support me?" he asked before taking a bite of his food. "I've done perfectly well on my own. I'm looking for a partner, not a servant."

"It's something Grandad used to pray for you." The ambient light from the chandelier hanging above them added to the sparkle in her blue eyes. "He said, and I quote, your brother's too hardheaded for his own good. He needs a kind and supportive woman to balance him out."

"That sounds like something he'd say, especially the hard-headed part."

"He was right, too. You could really use someone who'll balance you out. Someone who'll make you want to get out and do things other than work all day and night. Wouldn't that be great?"

"*Great* isn't the word I'm thinking of. Distracting's more like it."

Bekah drew her lips into a pout. "You're a lot less grumpy when Jace is around. I can't wait for him to finish touring and come home ..."

Devin couldn't agree more. Once Jace returned, Bekah would have someone to hang out with. All *he* wanted was to be left in peace. It was frustrating enough with Scarlett pinging him every hour, asking if he'd picked his top three candidates yet. Now his sister couldn't stop talking about all the ways he was being a killjoy. He had a feeling the quiet he'd hoped to find at home this weekend was a pipe dream.

"You okay, Dev?"

He glanced up from his plate. The way Bekah looked at him made it hard to speak. The older she got, the more she resembled their mother. The similarities weren't only external. They were both kindhearted, innocent, and giving, often at their own expense. That's why he felt the extra need to protect his sister. It was the least he could do since he hadn't been able to protect his mom.

Swallowing hard, Devin pushed down the sadness rising in his chest. He quickly nodded. "Yeah, I'm fine. Just thinking about work."

He'd be better off focusing on business, something he could control. People, on the other hand, were unpredictable and messy —his family was proof of that. If only their father had remained faithful to their mother, she wouldn't have blamed herself and succumbed to her grief. Maybe his twin wouldn't have dropped out of college to become a rock star. Bekah would have had a female role model to look up to instead of being raised in a home with three males. And he wouldn't have had to grow up so quickly and become a caretaker for his siblings.

"You're always thinking about work, Dev," Bekah griped as she set her fork down. She made a face with her nose scrunched up as if she smelled something bad. He expected her to roll her eyes, but she took a deep breath instead. After she released it, she leaned forward in her chair, an eager smile on her lips. "Have you picked your dates yet? Scarlett's hoping to hear back from you soon."

"Not yet," he bristled, not caring for the added pressure. "I've been busy."

"I can help if you're on the fence. I happen to have a personal favorite."

"How do you even know who these women are?"

"Scarlett showed me their profiles. She wanted to make sure I approved of them."

"Because it's more important for her to get your approval than mine?" He couldn't keep the sarcasm out of his voice. "I make multimillion-dollar decisions on a regular basis. I think I'm more than qualified to pick a woman to date."

"This has nothing to do with being qualified or not. Of course, she wants your input; that's why she's been texting you about it, but you haven't bothered to reply. I was just trying to help her speed up the process. Her sisters already have their clients' first dates lined up."

"Why do I get the feeling Scarlett's more concerned with winning a bet than with helping me?"

"She wants to do both."

"Right. Of course, you'd say that."

"Because it's true. Scarlett's the sweetest person I know. She's total wife material. You'd be lucky to marry her."

He scoffed loudly. The sound soon turned into laughter, bouncing off the floor-to-ceiling windows and the marble floor.

What a preposterous idea! Him marrying Scarlett? He wouldn't mind someone with similar traits as her, but not her specifically. He balked. "Trust me, sis, that woman is not my type."

"She's so your type, especially looks-wise. You like brunettes."

"No, I don't. I prefer blondes."

"Since when?"

"Since always."

She gave him the eye roll he'd been waiting for. "I don't know why you're being so difficult."

"I'm not being difficult." He stuffed his mouth with a forkful of pot pie, thankful for a reprieve from talking. This conversation was getting ridiculous. Why was he arguing with his sister about such a nonessential topic? "You're making this a bigger deal than it is. Like I said, Scarlett is not my type."

"Okay, if you say so. I suppose it's just as well, considering you're not her type at all either."

Devin paused mid-chew and eyed Bekah. "What makes you say that?"

"That's what Scarlett said." She narrowed her eyes at him until a grin curved her lips. "You don't look so happy, Dev. Are you offended?"

"Offended? Of course not. Why would I be offended? Everyone's entitled to their own opinion, whether it's accurate or not," he mumbled under his breath. He tossed his napkin onto the table. "I've got some work to do. I'll be in my office."

With a single shove of his chair, he pushed back from the table and rose to his feet. He turned to go, leaving Bekah gawking at him. She wasn't the only one confused. As much as he hated to admit it, she was right. He *was* offended by the news that he wasn't Scarlett's type. Why? He didn't know. But he wasn't desperate enough to give it any more thought.

And maybe if he told himself that a couple more times, he'd start to believe it.

CHAPTER 8
Scarlett

"That's when he got up and left the table!"

Scarlett listened to her friend describe Devin's reaction from earlier that evening as they hung out on the couch in the Kendalls' living room. As Bekah had promised, they were having girls' night at her place, complete with facial masks, sweets, and pedicures. For the past hour, they had gabbed and giggled like two teenagers. For Scarlett, this was the perfect way to unwind at the end of a long work week. Hearing that her disinterest in Devin had struck a nerve was as satisfying as icing on top of a cake.

Quite literally, too.

Scarlett took a bite of one of the cinnamon rolls she and Bekah had made earlier. She licked some icing off her upper lip and sighed with contentment. "I wish I could've seen your brother's face when you told him he's not my type."

"He was so offended! He acted like you'd personally insulted him. Well, I guess you pretty much did." Bekah's nose wrinkled beneath her gold-colored paper mask. "But he did insult you first by saying you're not *his* type."

"I'm not insulted at all. I don't expect to be every guy's type.

That's not how people and relationships work. If it were that easy to find someone to be compatible with, my family and I would be out of business."

"That's so true. It's like what we learned in Human Physiology class. Only 7% of the US population has a O negative blood type and can donate blood to anyone. My brother only wishes he were a universal match for all women."

Scarlett grinned. "Look at you getting all fancy with your science talk. I'm so glad you found something you enjoy studying."

"I really do. I finally feel like I know what I want to do with my life. I can't wait to graduate next June and become a full-fledged physical therapist."

"You're gonna be awesome at it, Dr. Kendall."

"Dr. Kendall—that has a nice ring to it, doesn't it?"

"It sure does." Knowing how hard Bekah had been working to achieve her goal made Scarlett feel like a proud older sister. "We should have a toast to your success so far. You know what would go well with this cinnamon roll?"

"Something bubbly?"

"Hot chocolate! My sisters and I always made hot chocolate when we had movie nights growing up."

"I love how your family had all these traditions." Bekah's tone grew wistful. "Growing up with brothers is such a different experience."

"I can only imagine. But don't worry, I'm here to help remedy that." She reached over and squeezed Bekah's arm. "Why don't you pick out a movie and I'll make the hot chocolate?"

"I can help. You don't know where everything is in the kitchen."

Scarlett handed her the remote as she stood up. "Your toenails are still wet. You stay put and relax. I've got this."

"Okay, thanks, Scar!"

With slow steps, Scarlett padded on her bare feet out of the living room, careful not to ruin her own fresh coat of toenail polish. When she passed a large oval mirror in the hallway, she happened to catch a glimpse of her reflection. With her hair held back in two braids and frog-print pajamas on, she looked about ready for bed. It was a good thing Bekah had asked her to sleep over tonight, so she could turn in as soon as the movie was over. She'd had a long week of work, but not only due to her day job.

Unknown to her family and friends, she did book narration on the side. Once upon a time, she'd wanted to become an actress, but she'd neither had the confidence nor her parents' support to pursue it beyond small roles in school productions. She'd prayed however for a way to use her skills and God had opened the door for her to narrate audiobooks. After some online research, she'd learned how to set up a makeshift studio in her bedroom closet and began offering her services online. She now had narrated more than a dozen books under a pseudonym and had more projects lined up. It was a dream come true for her to be doing something she loved, but it came with a price. She had to sacrifice sleep and cut out dairy products and sweets, the latter of which were not good for her throat. But she was gladly taking a break tonight and making an exception.

Scarlett picked up her pace as she entered the kitchen, eager to start making the hot chocolate. She stopped in her tracks at the sight of a man with damp hair, standing at the counter with his back to her. An impressive-looking back wearing a fitted short-sleeve shirt that showed off his broad shoulders and toned biceps. Muscles she didn't know existed rippled as he reached into a cabinet for a glass. His movements were swift and purposeful as he took a carton of milk from the fridge and poured some for himself.

She stood rooted in place, unable to tear her gaze away. Seeing Devin wearing something other than his suit and tie sparked a curiosity in her. Maybe it was the idea that he had a life outside of the office. It could also be the fact that he looked good, too good.

He'd been telling the truth about exercising every day. A body like that didn't appear out of thin air. Especially that backside. Whoever invented the form-fitting shorts he wore should have attached a warning label to them: May cause unwarranted heart palpitations.

Scarlett quickly forced her gaze away. What was she doing? She shouldn't be checking out her client! Moreover, her cheeks shouldn't be flushed as if *she* were the one who'd been working out!

Get a grip, Scarlett. You might be physically attracted to Devin, but that's all this is. She repeated these words to herself as she fanned her burning cheeks. Work—that's what she needed to focus on! And what better time to talk to Devin about his potential matches than now?

"Hey, Devin," she called out as she walked over. "Fancy meeting you here."

Devin turned around, the lower half of his face hidden by his milk. His brows shot up as he finished taking a gulp. He set the half-empty glass on the counter. "What are you doing here?"

"Bekah and I are having a girls' night in. She didn't tell you?"

"She failed to mention it at dinner." His blue eyes gave her a quick once-over. "Is there something you need?"

She smiled brightly. "Your three choices for your dates? Not that you have to give them to me right this minute, but sometime this evening would be nice."

"I was going to email them to you after my workout," he replied, his expression stoic. "That's not the only reason why you're in the kitchen, is it, to make sure I followed through on your request?"

She chewed her lower lip, not appreciating his bristling energy one bit. Bekah hadn't been joking about him being offended, but she was still put off by his attitude. Or did he not like to be surprised? She could understand the latter reason, but it wasn't like she'd come uninvited. Hopefully he was just caught off guard. On second thought, the way he was acting was pretty much how he behaved all the time. This wasn't anything new, but Scarlett had hoped they were on better terms after their meeting at her office.

Only a few days ago, they'd laughed and traded personal stories about their pasts. She'd even accidentally called him hot! That should've earned her some brownie points. But no, here they were back at square one again.

Sighing, she prayed for patience and self-control. She realized she'd been praying for the fruit of the Spirit a lot lately. That was without a doubt the only good thing to come about from meeting this infuriating man.

"No, I didn't know you'd be here," she replied. "I came to make hot chocolate for Bekah and myself."

"Hot chocolate? That's cute and rather appropriate." He stepped aside and nodded toward the milk sitting on the counter. "Help yourself."

"I will, thank you."

He grunted in response and returned to drinking.

Scarlett grabbed the carton and brought it closer. As she took two mugs from a cabinet, she wondered what he meant by *that's cute*. The word *cute* had always rubbed her the wrong way. Growing up, people always called her cute, whereas her older sisters were referred to as smart, strong, or pretty. Being seen as cute might be a compliment to some people, but for Scarlett, it was the last thing she wanted. She knew she ought to keep her mouth shut, but her pride wouldn't let this go.

Planting her hands on her hips, she spun around to face Devin. "What did you mean by *that's cute*?"

He lowered his glass. "I didn't mean anything by it."

"But you did. You wouldn't have said it otherwise. There's a reason you said *that's cute and rather appropriate*." She held his gaze without blinking. "What was it?"

"The real question," he challenged her, "is why does what I said bother you so much?"

"If you must know, I hate it when people use the word *cute*. When you're the youngest of four, you hear that word a lot. *You're so cute. Aren't you the cute baby sister? Look at the cute thing Scarlett's doing.* That word always made me feel like a little kid, like no one ever took me seriously." She blew out a heavy breath that sent some wayward strands of her hair flying. Now that she'd addressed the elephant in the room, she felt better. But a little worse, too. So much for having self-control and not letting Devin get to her. "Sorry, I didn't mean to bite your head off. It's just a big pet peeve of mine."

One side of his mouth lifted into a smirk. "It's a good thing I kept my reasoning to myself then."

Scarlett balked. "You can't say that now and not tell me what you meant!"

"Oh, yes, I can. I believe in self-preservation."

"So you did say *that's cute and appropriate* as an insult?"

"Not exactly."

"What does *not exactly* mean exactly?"

"It depends."

"It depends? What is that supposed to mean?" Shaking her head, Scarlett threw up her hands. Why did every conversation with Devin make her want to pull her hair out? "Never mind. It doesn't matter. Forget I asked."

He answered her with a raised brow.

"I'm gonna go make hot chocolate now. Thanks for the milk. And for sending me your choices later," she added with a terse smile before heading for the pantry.

With some distance between them, she could finally breathe freely. At least she kind of ended the conversation on a positive note, which was more than she could say for the emotions brewing in her gut. The rest of her evening would surely get better. As long as she steered clear of Devin Kendall, she'd be fine.

She hoped.

Scarlett marveled at the size and orderliness of the walk-in pantry. It was larger than her bedroom closet that she used as a makeshift recording studio. She looked up and down the shelves that had been stocked with a variety of goods until she spotted what she was searching for. There on the top shelf sat the hot cocoa powder just out of reach.

Oh, the woes of being height-challenged. That was another thing she'd hated as a child, not being as tall or as strong as her sisters. But no matter, she'd figured out how to get things done back then, and she'd figure out a way now.

She stood on her tiptoes, stretching her arm as far as it would go. Her fingernails scraped the round canister, but she couldn't get a firm hold on it. Frustration tightened her shoulder muscles when she realized she was about as helpless as a fish on dry land.

Unless she could find a stepstool! There had to be one somewhere. With renewed determination, Scarlett spun around, only to come face to face with Devin.

Great. He was the absolute last person she wanted help from. How long he'd been watching her from the doorway, she didn't know, but judging from his smug smile, it was obviously long enough.

"Need some help?" he asked.

Now just how badly did she want that cocoa?

CHAPTER 9
Devin

Devin leaned against the doorframe, his hands stuffed into his shorts pockets. He'd witnessed Scarlett's meager attempts at getting the cocoa powder and had to fight hard to keep from laughing. The characteristic she'd said she disliked was the very one she embodied. Despite being a grown woman, she was the essence of cute. With her braids and those ridiculous pj's on, not to mention her pouty expression, she possessed an air of innocence bordering on naivety. Of course, he wouldn't say this to her face. She seemed to have enough of a complex as it was. He would try his best to hold back his laughter for as long as possible.

She crossed her arms, covering up the cartoon frog on her chest. "Are you going to stand there and laugh at me all night or are you going to help?"

"Who said I was laughing?"

"The least you can do is admit to it." Her cheeks pinkened. "People like you have no idea what it's like to be in my shoes."

"People like me?" Why did this feel like a personal attack? "What's that supposed to mean?"

"You're tall. I bet you've never had to ask for help to get something that was out of reach."

"I haven't, but only because I prefer not to ask. Why ask for help when you can figure things out on your own? Where there's a will, there's a way." He gestured to his left where a folding stepstool leaned against the wall. "There's a stepstool over there for this very purpose. If you'd taken the time to look, you wouldn't need my help."

Her hands moved down to her hips as she widened her stance. "I was just about to look for one when you showed up. But since you offered to help, I'll take you up on it." She paused and furrowed her brows. "Why are you so against asking for help? Are you too proud?"

He sneered at the twinkle lighting up her green eyes. If she was trying to provoke him for laughing at her, she'd need to try harder. He wasn't so easily shaken. He'd been called worse things by his own father. His skin had grown far too thick for him to be affected by anyone's words, much less Scarlett's. "What if I am?" he touted boldly. "That's how I got to where I am. You don't become a CEO by being weak."

"But you do by being lonely." Her voice softened. "I understand now why you haven't met anyone yet. You won't let people get close to you. You have this wall built up to keep them out. It might protect you from getting hurt, but it keeps you from experiencing good things like love and companionship."

Devin flinched. Her words hit a little too close to home. The fact that he could no longer control his body's visceral reactions attested to this. How was she able to pinpoint his struggles so quickly and easily? She also had no qualms about telling the truth to his face.

She wasn't like other women who tried to impress him and get on his good side with flowery compliments. Scarlett had guts—he'd give her that. Even though she might appear naive on the outside, she possessed an inner strength and confidence that warranted respect. Devin hated to say it, but she wasn't wrong about him. He'd never had a meaningful, long-term relationship built on trust and transparency. But was he going to admit this to her? Not a chance.

He took two long strides over to where she waited with her back against the shelves. Reaching up, he plucked the container off the top shelf and brought it down. That's when his gaze fell to hers and he realized how close they were standing. He could feel the warmth of her breath on his skin as her lips parted. A hint of cinnamon lingered in the air between them, along with the light floral scent of her shampoo. But it was her wide-eyed stare that grabbed his attention and made his mouth go dry.

Those bright green eyes mesmerized him. The openness and trust they held unlocked something deep within. In Scarlett's eyes, he found a reflection of happier days. Back when life had been carefree, and contentment had been within reach. A time when his belief in God had been simple and pure. In her eyes, he saw hope. For a moment, he felt it, too, and almost longed for it ... until reality literally yanked him back to the present.

Scarlett took the container of cocoa from his hand. "I've got it. Thanks."

He shook his head free from his wayward thoughts and immediately stepped aside to put some distance between them. "I have work to do." Then he shoved his hands into his pockets again and walked away.

It wasn't until he reached his office on the other side of the house that he breathed freely. What had happened? He'd never been so caught off guard before by a woman. If she hadn't taken the cocoa from him, who knows how long he would have stood there staring? He didn't like this feeling coursing through him, this sense of confusion. Why had he been drawn to Scarlett like that? He couldn't possibly be attracted— No, that was out of the question.

She was a beautiful woman, but they were like oil and water.

They couldn't even have a conversation without offending each other. She'd rubbed him the wrong way more times than he could count. Scarlett was a ball of fire in a pretty little package. She infuriated him like no other ... yet she also intrigued him beyond reason.

Why did You bring this woman into my life, God?!

Annoyance rushed through his veins, sending his blood pressure soaring. How was he supposed to get any work done now?

It'd been years since he'd felt this out of control, and he hated it. Hated it so much that he almost felt the desire to ask God for help. But he hadn't done so in a long, long time. It wasn't that he didn't believe in a higher power, he just wasn't used to relying on someone other than himself. The fact that he was even entertaining the idea irked him. How was it that one woman could mess with his head like this? This was further proof that he needed to watch himself around Scarlett.

Once seated at his desk, Devin threw his head back and shut his eyes. He massaged his temples to ward off the migraine threatening to take over. That's when his cell phone rang.

His brother's name flashed across the screen. "Hey, Jace," he answered. "You doing okay?"

"Hey, bro." Jace's enthusiastic voice rose over the loud din on his end of the line. He was likely on a tour bus with his bandmates traveling to their next destination. "I should be asking you that question. Something tells me you're not doing so hot."

Devin smirked. He'd never believed in the twin telepathy talk that Jace swore by, but there had been too many instances like this one that made him wonder if any of it was true. "I'm fine. Just have a lot on my plate."

"It's Friday night. You should be out with a girl, not sitting at home in front of your computer."

He stared at his reflection in the monitor across from him, bemused. "How did you know where I'm sitting?"

"You're always at your computer. If you were anywhere else, I'd be worried you'd hit your head and gotten amnesia."

"That doesn't sound like a bad thing right now." If he lost his memory, he'd at least have some peace, if only temporarily. His cousin's threats to take over the company hung in the forefront of his mind like a wrecking ball he couldn't dodge. He knew he should act quickly and find a wife, but the more he considered his options, the more he dreaded going out with those women. If he didn't want to date any of them, how could he imagine marrying one?

"What's going on, Dev? Talk to me."

The last thing he wanted was to burden his brother with his problems. Jace was the carefree one; he had concerts to play and fans to entertain. He'd always had fewer expectations placed upon him by their father. As the older twin, Devin had known from a young age that he was to take on the family business one day. They might have been born only eight minutes apart, but the difference between their responsibilities was as far as the east was from the west. Jace wouldn't understand his struggle even if he did know about it. "It's nothing. Just dealing with headaches at work as usual."

"Work, work, work. When are you going to do something else with your time? Work will always be there, but your youth won't be. You should go out and meet people, get a little action in. Come on, Dev. With a face like yours, you can get any woman you want. I should know," he added with a chuckle.

Devin shook his head in wonder. He and Jace might be identical in their DNA, but that's where the similarities ended. "I see you've been enjoying yourself on the road," he drawled with disapproval. "How many hearts have you broken this week?"

"None. They were all more than happy to have spent time with me."

The confidence in Jace's smooth voice concerned him. When would he ever learn? "Just keep yourself out of trouble, will you?

The last thing you want is one of those women to show up with a kid that she says is yours."

"You worry too much, bro."

"Maybe you should worry a little more." His next breath came out as a long sigh. Great—his head throbbed even more now, which often happened when he talked with Jace. The best thing to do was to finish his work, take a hot shower, and go to bed. "Thanks for calling, but if there's nothing else, I need to get back to work."

"There is one thing, Dev. It's about Bekah."

"What about her?"

"She told me she's been hanging out with Bash. She says it's for school, but something tells me there's more going on. You know she always had a crush on him."

Devin's jaw clenched. Bash had been the neighbor kid growing up and a troublemaker. He wasn't the type of guy their sister should be falling for. "Thanks for letting me know. I'll talk to her."

"Cool. I know she'll listen to you."

A soft knock drew his gaze to the open door of his office. That's where he spotted those green eyes he'd been staring into just moments ago. Devin swallowed hard. What was Scarlett doing here?

CHAPTER 10
Scarlett

Scarlett hadn't planned on seeing Devin again that evening. After their awkward encounter in the pantry, she'd been more than relieved when he'd left her alone in the kitchen.

Maybe she'd said too much earlier and had been too frank with him. She never imagined seeing such a different side to Devin. The sad, vulnerable look in his eyes had made her defenses crack enough for her to feel ashamed of her actions.

She'd basically called him lonely and proud for not wanting help. The irony of the situation was that she'd also been too proud to ask him for help.

While she loved pie, humble pie was not one she enjoyed swallowing. But the Lord had been poking at her heart and helping her to see the plank in her own eye. Now He was giving her a chance to make things right. Hopefully, Devin would be more gracious with her than she'd been with him. But even if he wasn't, she was ready to play nice.

When he gestured for her to enter, she walked over, holding the mugs of hot chocolate she'd prepared a few minutes ago. "Bekah fell asleep, so I was wondering if you'd like her hot cocoa?" The moment she set his mug down, she noticed he was on the phone. Lowering her volume, she added, "I'll just leave it here for you."

Devin held up his hand to stop her from leaving. "Have a seat, Scarlett." He then murmured into the phone, "It's not what you think, Jace."

Scarlett nodded, surprised. For a second, she'd thought she could get away without apologizing, but it seemed God wasn't letting her off the hook that easily. It was just as well. Character-building wasn't supposed to be easy. If only it didn't have to be so humbling, too.

She turned around to give Devin some privacy and tried her best to not eavesdrop, even though a big part of her wanted to. There was still more about him that remained a mystery, apart from what Bekah had told her. But Bekah, being so much younger than her brothers, only knew so much. His twin, Jace, would be the perfect person to talk to. Too bad she couldn't listen in on their conversation.

Forcing her feet to move, she crossed to the other side of the room and sat down on the leather couch. Taking a sip of her cocoa, she glanced around the office in wonder. The large space had a stately feel to it with a mahogany desk and wooden floor-to-ceiling shelves built into the walls. Small circular end tables with intricate designs carved into the tabletops sat on either side of her. Situated diagonally from the couch was the only piece of modern furniture in the room—a reclining chaise lounge chair. It looked like a reader's paradise with a knit blanket draped across the back. There was a hardcover lying on top that beckoned her over.

Intrigued by the familiar cover, Scarlett walked over and picked it up. Just as she'd suspected, it was one of the true crime books she'd narrated about a year ago. She and the author worked so well together, she went on to narrate several more in the same series. In fact, the audiobook she was currently recording was for a new book that would be releasing next month. Scarlett wondered if Devin had listened to any of them, and if so, whether he'd recognized her voice.

"Have you read it?"

Scarlett inhaled sharply at the sound of Devin's deep voice. She hadn't realized he had gotten off the phone already. But now that he was standing beside her, his masculine scent filling her senses, there was no denying his presence. Or the unfortunate way her heart thumped in her chest to be so close to him again. She took a step to the side as she glanced up. "I've read the whole series. They're even better as audiobooks."

He nodded, then gestured for them to sit. "There's something I want to talk to you about."

She followed him to the couch, thankful that he hadn't asked her to elaborate on her last comment. The words had slipped out before she could think them through. Regardless, there was a more important matter to address. She set her mug on the side table, then faced him. "If I may, I'd like to apologize to you first."

"What for?"

"For what I said earlier. I'll admit it, my attitude was wrong, and I just wanted to have the last word. I shouldn't have been so petty. I'm sorry." Once the apology was out, Scarlett felt a weight lift off her shoulders. She released a deep breath. "That wasn't as hard as I'd thought it'd be."

Devin's stoic expression gave way to a smirk. "I take it you don't apologize often."

"Not if I can help it. Do you like apologizing?"

"Not particularly. That might be the one thing we have in common."

Scarlett grinned at the amusement in his voice. "Other than wanting to prove the other person wrong? Don't tell me you don't find enjoyment in that?"

"Touché. It appears we have two things in common then."

"Who would've thought?"

His smile widened, showing off a set of perfectly straight teeth.

He leaned against the cushions and rested one arm along the back of the couch. His relaxed posture surprised Scarlett. Maybe the olive branch, or rather the hot chocolate, had done its job. She watched him take a sip and wondered what else she'd find out about him tonight.

"You said you wanted to talk to me about something," she began in a hopeful tone. "Is it about your dates?"

His expression turned serious. "It's about Bekah. Has she told you anything about a guy named Bash?"

"No, I'm pretty sure she hasn't."

"Do you know if she's been spending time with a male friend?"

Scarlett thought about her recent conversations with Bekah and shook her head. "All she talks about these days are her classes or what we learned from women's group. I'm sure if she were hanging out with a guy, she'd tell me about it. We've talked about guys before."

"Her and guys, or you and guys?"

"Both. We've even talked about you, Mr. Kendall. Nothing worth repeating though." His face remained serious despite her teasing tone. The only change she noticed was a muscle twitch along his jawline. He sure was a tough crowd to please. She reached over and gave his arm a playful pat. "Lighten up, Devin. It's okay to laugh at my jokes."

"I will when I find them to be funny." His smirk reappeared in full force, along with a twinkle that lit up his blue eyes.

"Ha ha. And to think that I was going to offer to get some intel on this Bash guy for you." She sighed dramatically. "Now you'll never know if or who Bekah's dating."

He gave her a pointed look. "I can talk to her myself. But if you care about her, you'll help me keep an eye out. Bash is not someone I want Bekah associating with."

Scarlett was taken aback at the intensity of his tone. "I'm sure you have a reason for feeling that way, but give your sister some credit. Bekah's smart. She wouldn't do anything rash."

"You have no idea what you're talking about." His voice was more somber than accusatory. "Love makes people do foolish things, oftentimes at their own expense."

His words brought up a slew of memories from the past, ones she preferred not to dwell on. At least God had healed her enough from the pain, so it didn't hurt as much now to talk about her regrets. "Unfortunately, I do understand more than you think. That's why I stayed with my ex for so long because I thought he loved me, and I loved him. I tried so hard to be the perfect girlfriend, then fiancée, by putting his needs first. I thought by doing so, he'd realize how much he needed me."

"And he'd finally wake up and appreciate you?"

"Yes. How did you know?"

His eyes took on a faraway look. "I knew someone like that. It didn't end well for her, and it obviously didn't work out for you either. That's why I have to protect Bekah from making the same mistake."

The bitterness in his voice was so heavy, she could almost taste it. Whoever he was talking about had to have meant a lot to him. This was the most vulnerable she'd ever seen him. Compassion stirred within her to know that underneath his gruff exterior, he had a soft heart, too.

Scarlett reached over and gave his arm a light squeeze. "You're a good brother. I can tell you care about Bekah very much."

He brushed off her compliment. "It's my responsibility."

"Not completely. She's a grown woman; she can take care of herself. But I get it—she's the youngest of the family and as her older sibling, you feel a sense of responsibility toward her. That's how it is with my sisters and me. It's very much a blessing and a curse to be the youngest."

Devin shook his head. "It's much worse being the oldest. You have no idea what we go through. We have so much more pressure and responsibilities."

"I could say the same about being the youngest. We're always lagging behind and having to prove ourselves to everyone we meet. Imagine going through school and having every single teacher compare you to your older siblings and being disappointed that you're not as smart or as strong or as pretty as they are. It's enough to give you a complex."

"You know what, the younger ones do have it worse."

Scarlett beamed, feeling like she'd just won. She didn't have a medal, ribbon, or crown to show for her victory like her sisters did, but the genuine smile on Devin's face was enough. She grabbed her mug and held it toward his. "This calls for a toast! To younger siblings who go through life with big footsteps to follow and their older siblings who leave them behind."

Devin clinked her mug with a hearty chuckle. "Cheers."

Later that night, Scarlett went to sleep believing more than ever that the Lord answered prayers. There was no other reason for how well she and Devin had gotten along because if it were up to her, she would rather fight than make peace. But God was obviously changing her heart. So much so that she found herself looking forward to the next time she'd see him again ... for purely professional reasons of course.

CHAPTER 11
Devin

Miniature golf or bowling—who did that?

Devin shook his head, thinking about the suggestions Scarlett had given him for his date tonight. That had been a week ago, and he still couldn't stop smiling every time he thought about her innocent green eyes. Her enthusiasm was so pure and unmatched; it was nearly contagious. Not enough for him to go along with her plan, but he found himself wondering if he should have. If he and his date had done an activity instead of going out to dinner, he at least would have something to keep him entertained. Because the silence between him and the woman sitting across the table was as thick as the Béarnaise sauce on his plate.

Moira, a CEO he thought he'd have the most in common with, couldn't stop glancing down at her phone. She wasn't even being discreet about it. Watching her check her emails had Devin itching to do the same, but Scarlett's five rules of etiquette wouldn't leave his mind.

1 - Put away your phone.
2 - Don't talk about your exes.
3 - Ask open-ended questions.

4 - Make eye contact without being creepy (her exact words, not his).

5 - Give her genuine compliments.

Fine. After all the preparation that Scarlett had done with him, he would at least do his part to give this date a shot. It wasn't like he didn't understand the struggles of being a CEO; he knew them full well. That's why he'd been biding his time and making an effort to be patient. His patience had a limit though, one he was nearing. There were other things he could be doing instead of wasting his efforts here.

"Looks like your work keeps you busy," he remarked as he tried again to make eye contact.

Moira's head of short blonde waves bobbed up and down as her fingers flew over her phone screen. "You have no idea! The board's been breathing down my neck over last quarter's numbers. And lately, I've been putting out one fire after another. I barely have time to eat, much less sleep."

"I can see that."

She glanced up for a split second with a sheepish smile. If Devin had a dollar for every time she'd done that this past hour, he'd have enough to pay for their meal.

Their fairly expensive meal.

He'd taken her to the nicest steak and seafood house in San Jose's Santana Row, yet she'd only taken two bites of her crab cakes. At the pace she was eating, they'd be here until closing.

Buzz!

His phone vibrated in his pocket, tempting him to check it. He'd resisted a multitude of times, but no more. What was the point when his date didn't care if he paid attention to her or not? He pulled it out and read the new texts lighting up the screen.

Hey, Mr. CEO, how's your date going? Isn't Moira so pretty and sweet?! I'm sure the two of you have so much to talk about!

Devin scoffed. He'd never seen so many exclamation points in one message. Despite Scarlett's enthusiasm, she couldn't be more wrong. So much for her professional matchmaking skills. He quickly typed out his reply.

I wouldn't know. She's been glued to her phone all night.

Scarlett responded immediately: *Devin! What happened to rule #1?! You're not supposed to be on your phone during your date!*

He paused, realizing her intentions.

Did you text me just to test me?

Yes! And you failed!! She added a smiling squinting face emoji.

I'll have you know that I refrained all evening. The person you really should be testing is my date, not me. Before hitting the send button, he searched for an appropriate emoji to reply with. Two could play this game.

I can't believe you're sticking your tongue out at me! But good choice! I didn't think you knew how to use emojis.

They're not hard to figure out. I could say the same for you. I didn't think you knew how to use periods at the end of your sentences.

Ha! You're pretty funny sometimes, Devin. You should show Moira how funny you are.

I honestly don't think she'd care. I'm about to stop caring, too. I have work that I could be doing right now.

Devin waited for Scarlett's reply, but none came. After a minute, however, Moira cleared her throat and began talking.

"I'm so sorry, Devin," she began in a stilted tone. "I didn't mean to leave you high and dry during our dinner together. I feel terrible. I would like to get to know you better if you'll give me the chance."

He glanced up, expecting to see Moira's trademark smile again, but she still had her eyes on her phone. She'd apparently been reading off her apology, one that Scarlett had no doubt written for her.

Devin didn't know whether to sneer or laugh. It was bad enough to be ignored by his date all night, but for her to not even know how to apologize to him was ludicrous!

He flagged down their server and paid for the bill. "It's obvious you don't want to be here, Moira, which is fine by me. I have things I need to do. It's time I put us both out of our misery. Have a good night," he added as he stood up and grabbed his jacket.

"Thanks for dinner!" Moira called out as he walked away.

The moment Devin got behind the wheel of his car, he dialed Scarlett's number. He was ready to give her an earful for this failure of a date.

She answered on the first ring. "Now, Devin, before you start griping about how much time you wasted tonight, hear me out."

Gritting his teeth, he replied, "I'm listening."

"But first, put me on speakerphone. You need your hands free to drive."

He couldn't roll his eyes fast enough. "I'm perfectly capable of driving and talking at the same time," he barked as he reluctantly switched the call over to his car's speakerphone. "I'm paying you to be my matchmaker, not my driving instructor."

"I know, but safety first! I need you to be in one piece for your next date tomorrow."

"Next date?" he repeated as he hightailed it out of the parking lot. "You've got to be kidding me. What makes you think I'm putting myself through this nonsense again? Whatever screening method you used to match me with Moira failed—miserably. We had nothing in common. There was no effort made on her part at all. I might as well have been talking to a wall. All she was concerned about was her job. She couldn't even apologize on her own; you had to feed her the words to say!"

"That was my sister Emerald's doing; Moira's her client. She is genuinely sorry though; she just needed help verbalizing it. She's not used to apologizing, something I know you're familiar with. See, you two do have something in common."

Devin could hear a smile in Scarlett's voice, but it did nothing to appease him. In fact, her cavalier attitude made him scowl even more. He stepped on the gas, enjoying the rush of adrenaline that coursed through his body now that he was on the move again. "If you're trying to be funny, I'd advise you not to quit your day job. Actually, I take that back. If my date tonight was any reflection on your matchmaking skills, you'd be better off reconsidering your career choice."

A soft sigh came over the line, followed by silence. When Scarlett failed to speak, Devin wondered if he'd been too harsh. He'd been warned by HR more than once to watch his tone. After three of his Executive Assistants quit in the span of a year, he could no longer deny that he shared some responsibility in the matter.

Some responsibility, not all.

Not everyone could meet his standards, but was that his fault? When had it become wrong to demand excellence?

"All right," Scarlett finally piped up, "I assume you're done griping, Mr. CEO? If so, it's my turn to say my piece."

Devin blinked, completely caught off guard. Not only had Scarlett not been offended by his spiel, but she was ready to give him hers? What sorry excuse would she come up with to defend her lack of experience? "Go on."

"I did exactly what you asked for, Devin. I offered Moira as a candidate because you said you wanted someone driven and independent. She fit the bill perfectly. The reason the two of you didn't click is not because you don't have anything in common; on the contrary, you have too much in common. You're both go-getters and overachievers and both in need of someone who will offer you what you can't offer to each other."

"And what is that?"

"Support and peace. A sense of home if you will. You need someone to pull you away from work, not toward it."

He clenched his hands on the steering wheel, not knowing whether to be impressed or annoyed. Who did Scarlett think she was—a shrink? And how did someone her age have the gall to be lecturing him about what he needed? Didn't he know himself better than she did?

Apparently not.

What she'd said wasn't wrong. She made a lot of sense, but he wasn't in the mood to admit defeat, especially not out loud. While he felt somewhat bad for giving her a hard time, he only allowed himself a low humph.

Scarlett filled the lull with a soft chuckle. "I know you agree with me, Devin, but you want to plead the Fifth. It's fine, you've had a long week of work and a not-so-ideal evening. I'm really proud of you for doing things that were out of your comfort zone tonight like putting your phone away and doing something fun—although it didn't end up to be all that fun. But tomorrow's a new day with a new opportunity to try again. I guarantee you that tomorrow's match will be more compatible for you."

"You guarantee it? That's bold of you to claim. What if she isn't?"

"Well, let me add in a disclaimer: I promise the date will go off without a hitch if you agree to take her miniature golfing."

"You've got to be kidding—"

"I'm serious, Devin. Trust me on this. Just give it a try. What have you got to lose?"

"Other than my reputation?"

A peal of laughter erupted over the line. "You're being so dramatic! I'm not asking you to dress up like a clown and dance around the course. It's a game of golf. All you have to do is hit a ball into a hole."

"I know what golf is and how to play. The problem is ..." Clenching his jaw tight, he hesitated to answer. Why did he have to justify himself in front of Scarlett anyway? He ought to be able to say no without needing to elaborate on the details.

"Yes? What's the problem?"

"It makes no sense. What is the point of doing an activity that keeps you so preoccupied you wouldn't be able to carry on a decent conversation at the same time? Isn't that the whole point of a date, to get to know the other person? I won't be able to do that and focus on the game."

"Ohh, I see."

Her mysterious tone irritated him. "What do you see?"

"Do you ever do anything for fun, Devin? Or is everything a competition for you?"

"What kind of question is that?"

"It's just that the way you were describing miniature golf makes it sound like you care an awful lot about winning the game."

"Of course, I do. Why else would I play?"

"How about for enjoyment? To have a chance to observe your date and find out more about her? Or maybe even to consider cheering her on and learning how not to be a sore loser if she wins? These are all rhetorical questions, in case you can't tell."

He tapped his fingers impatiently. "I'm not dull, Scarlett; I know they're rhetorical."

"And I know you're not dull. I'm willing to bet my other eyebrow that you're a whole lotta fun on the inside. But just in case," she mused with a smile in her voice, "I'd like you to meet me an hour before your date tomorrow, so I can give you a few pointers."

"Oh really? On golfing or dating?"

"Both! You know matchmaking's in my blood, but what you don't know is that I'm a golf prodigy. I advise you to bring your A game tomorrow, Mr. Kendall."

"You're on, Ms. Hayes."

"Great! I'll see you then! Good night."

The call ended with Scarlett's bright voice replaying in Devin's mind, along with the surprising realization that he might be looking forward to tomorrow's date.

CHAPTER 12
Scarlett

Scarlett's first reaction when she saw Devin the next afternoon was one of surprise. He was dressed rather appropriately for this date. Not that she'd thought he would show up in work attire, but she hadn't expected him to look so casual—or handsome. She had a hard time tearing her gaze away as he strode over from the parking lot to the entrance of the miniature golf course.

His navy checked chino pants fit him like a second skin and his white short-sleeved polo shirt complemented his tanned skin so well. How someone who stayed in the office all day managed to look so sun-kissed was beyond her. All she knew was that Devin would have no problem impressing his date with his appearance. Now it was up to her to help him with the rest of the package.

Easier said than done.

If only she hadn't stayed up till almost 3 a.m. trying to finish her narration work. She stifled the yawn threatening to escape her lips and pushed out a bright smile. She might not be feeling like her usual peppy self, but she'd fake it till she made it. "Hey, Mr. CEO, you look rather dashing today. I'm glad you left the suit and tie at home."

"I can't play well if I'm not comfortable." He gave her a quick once-over. "You look different."

"Different how?" Feeling self-conscious, Scarlett glanced down at her chambray shirt that she wore over a red-striped maxi dress. She'd been bleary-eyed when she'd gotten dressed that morning, so it was possible she'd buttoned up her top wrong. It looked fine, though. She spotted a smile playing on Devin's lips. "What is it? Do I have something on my face?"

He pointed down at the ground. "Your shoes. They're mismatched."

She gasped when she saw a sandal on her left foot and a canvas slip-on on her right. At least they were both white. "I promise you I'm a lot more put-together on the inside than I am on the outside. I had a late night."

"I hope that doesn't mean you're going to take it easy on me. I came prepared." He gestured to the lightweight golf bag hanging from his shoulder.

"You brought your own club for miniature golf?"

"Just a putter."

"A what-er?"

"A putter. You use it to hit the ball short distances. It's similar to what they rent here." He eyed her warily. "Didn't you claim to be an expert at golf?"

"I am ... at Mario Golf. I never said I played in person." She flashed him a cheeky smile. "Come on, let's go! It's time to start your lesson!"

She led the way through the double doors of Golfland's main building with Devin chuckling behind her. The familiar lights and sounds of the arcade games surrounded them as they headed over to the cashier. Two small girls ran about, giggling as their parents followed. Seeing those kids reminded Scarlett of the many times she'd come here with her own family when she was younger. She'd never, however, gone miniature golfing on a date before.

Not that this was a date.

That thought shouldn't have even crossed her mind. She was strictly here for work. Except that this was the oddest thing she'd ever done on the job. She normally didn't go on-site with a client, especially not a male one.

Now that she was here, she realized she may have crossed a line when she'd told Devin to meet her early. She'd been so caught up in their fun banter, she'd wanted to keep it going. And as a competitive person herself, she'd really wanted to go head-to-head with him on the golf course. But it was time to dial things back and make sure her mind was focused on business and business alone.

Please help me not to be distracted, Lord!

Devin was the first one to hand over his credit card to the gum-chewing young man at the register. "I've got this."

His offer surprised Scarlett, but she was just as fast. Pushing her credit card across the counter, she insisted, "I'll pay for my ticket."

"I said I've got this."

"You should save your money for your date."

"Trust me, money is not an issue for me." His smirk softened as he added, "My mother taught me women should be treated with care and respect. I always pay."

"I'm glad you do and I'm sure the women you pay for are grateful, but this isn't a date. I can pay my share."

"Didn't you call this a dating lesson? If I'm here to practice dating, I should practice paying, too." Without another word, Devin urged the cashier to ring them up.

Scarlett reluctantly took her card and followed Devin out with their balls and her club in hand. When she caught up with him at the gate to the courses, she remarked through gritted teeth, "Thank you for paying."

"The pleasure's all mine."

She wrinkled her nose, not appreciating the victorious twinkle in his eye. "You really like to win at everything, don't you?"

"Don't you?"

"That's not—" Scarlett cut herself off, feeling more frustrated at herself than at Devin. She couldn't afford to let him get under her skin right now. They didn't have much time left before his date arrived, and there was obviously a lot they needed to go over. She took a deep breath before trusting herself to speak again. "Okay, here's a new rule. Rule number six—listen to your date. I appreciate that chivalry isn't dead in your world, but sometimes a girl might have a good reason for wanting to pay her own way."

"Other than not wanting to lose an argument?"

His wry tone was hard to miss. "Yes," she replied as graciously as possible. "But if not wanting to lose an argument happens to be the only reason, it's still enough reason to back down. That's also a way to show a woman respect."

He nodded, albeit reluctantly. "You have a point."

"Thank you." She beamed, happy he'd come around without a fight. "I must say, you're a quick learner."

"That's because you're a good teacher." He lowered his voice and added, "That was for rule number five, in case you're keeping score."

She rolled her eyes. "It only works when it's a genuine compliment."

"That was genuine. I do think you're a good teacher, especially for having to deal with a student like me. I know I can be hard-headed sometimes."

"Sometimes?" She clamped her lips together before she got into more trouble. "I mean, aren't we all? I'll admit I have a bit of a stubborn streak myself."

"I know." He grinned widely. "I appreciate you owning up to it."

Scarlett balked. She had no words. She'd lost her train of thought as soon as he laughed. It was the most genuine smile she'd seen on him, complete with crinkles at the corners of his ocean-blue eyes. His deep, rich laugh did something to her insides that she couldn't control or ignore. Before she could react, Devin began walking toward the advanced course, the one farthest from them.

He turned around and waved. "Are you coming or are you going to forfeit the game?"

"Not a chance! Only losers forfeit!" She shuffled her feet, moving as fast as possible with her mismatched shoes. Hopefully her game would be more on point than her footwear because she was determined to win. As soon as she stepped up to the first hole, however, an unsettled feeling tugged at her heart.

What was she doing?

She was supposed to prepare Devin for his date, not put him in his place, no matter how much she wanted to. This was no time to play games—other than golf. She needed to put her pride aside and remember her purpose—to get her client matched and married. Thankfully, that wouldn't be much harder to accomplish than winning at golf.

Scarlett was coming to see that Devin Kendall had his strong suits. Sure, he came off a little rough around the edges, but the more time they spent together, the more she appreciated about him. He was hardworking and quick-witted, and he had a good sense of humor. And somewhere deep, deep, deep inside of him was a heart that actually cared. The way he watched out for his siblings and made it a point to treat women with respect proved he had a soft side. It didn't hurt that he was very easy on the eyes, especially when he smiled.

He really was the whole package. Which meant she had no excuse to fail at this assignment.

"Change of plans!" she exclaimed. "We're both going to forfeit the game."

"Excuse me?" His brows drew together as he frowned. "You were the one who told me to bring my A game, and now you want me to lose?"

"Let me explain. What I want is for both of us to win. I would be doing you a great disservice if I focused more on the game than on helping you prepare for your date, which is exactly what I didn't want you to be doing. It's time for a course correction. We're going to focus more on talking and less on playing."

"What was the point of coming to a golf course then?"

"So you and your date won't be glued to your phones."

"I wasn't the one on the phone last night."

"Touché. I meant so your date won't be tempted to be on her phone."

He grinned. "That's more like it. So, I'm not supposed to win at golf, but I should win at the game of communication."

"Yes, exactly! That way she'll see what an amazing person you are and fall madly in love with you and want to marry you and have your babies. And one day, when those babies are older, you can bring them here and tell them all about the time you met their mom at Golfland and how you impressed her with your swings and, more importantly, with your awesome conversational skills. That'll be some story to tell, won't it?"

"You left out the most important part."

"What's that?"

Squinting against the sunshine, she glanced up, expecting him to make some kind of smart-alecky comment. Instead, he placed his hand next to her forehead to shield her from the sun's rays. The gesture was surprisingly thoughtful and sweet. Despite the shadow that fell over her, she felt a warmth flood her chest. She could look into his face with ease now, but the tender expression she saw there made it hard to breathe.

"You forgot to mention yourself."

CHAPTER 13
Devin

Maybe he had said too much?

Devin dropped his hand, shocked at the truth of his words. In the most inexplicable, unexpected way, Scarlett Hayes had become an important part of this journey.

Perhaps even his life.

Emotions he'd never experienced before swelled in his chest. He couldn't look at her without feeling hope and—dare he say it—joy. She was the most interesting woman he'd ever met. No other person could make him roll his eyes and laugh in the same breath. No one else made him feel so alive.

And yet, he seemed to have the opposite effect on her.

The way she stared at him, her mouth agape and eyes open wide, was not the reaction any man wanted from a woman he'd just opened up to. Scarlett not only looked surprised, she seemed horrified.

Yes, he had definitely said too much.

"I meant that without you," he explained matter-of-factly, "there would be no marriage or children to speak of. You are the matchmaker, after all."

"Oh!" Her expression brightened as she laughed. "Of course,

that's what you meant. Well, it is my job, you know. I'm all about making sure my clients get their happy ever after. That's why you hired me, right?"

Devin grunted in agreement. Hired—that one word spoke volumes. Theirs was a working relationship, nothing more. Scarlett spent time with him because she had to, not because she liked his company. If their time together had proven anything, it was how much he frustrated her. No wonder she seemed so eager to put some distance between them.

Scarlett now stood to his side about three feet away, pointing her golf putter at him like a weapon. She waved him forward. "Why don't you start?"

Devin studied her expression, wishing he could read her thoughts. There was so much he didn't know about her. All this time, he had been the one talking about himself, about his needs and his wants. For the first time since he met Scarlett, he wanted to learn about her. Who was this woman who was able to get him to let his guard down so easily? What were her needs and what did she want?

As with any goal he decided on that was worth pursuing, he made up his mind in that moment to find out more about Scarlett. And he'd use this game of golf to do just that.

"I usually say ladies first," he replied, "but in the spirit of rule number six, I'll go first. But there is something I would like to propose to make this game more interactive, since that is the goal of our meeting today."

Scarlett's brows rose. "Are you trying to do my job now?"

"I'm merely making a suggestion."

"Okay, let's hear it."

"For every hole in one we hit, we get to ask the other person a question."

"Hmm." She pursed her lips as she thought. "You're trying to make this interactive and competitive? I can get on board with that. The only thing I don't like is that I didn't come up with the idea first."

"How about I give you partial credit? I'm sure you've rubbed off on me these past couple of weeks with all the advice you've been giving."

"That's really good to hear, especially given our—how shall I put it—challenging start." Her green eyes lit up with humor. "I guess it's true what they say—you can teach an old dog new tricks."

"Are you calling me old now?"

"I meant mature."

"Aren't I only a couple of years older than you?"

"A couple is two. You're half a decade older. When I was born, you were already learning your ABCs."

"Actually, I started reading when I was four. By age five, I'd already taught myself how to play the piano."

Her jaw dropped. "I change my mind. You are old. How did you teach yourself to read music?"

He held up a hand and shook his head. "No questions until you get a hole in one."

"Okay, fine. Hurry up then, Grandpa! I want my turn!"

If anyone else had called him Grandpa, Devin would have put them in their place. Yet Scarlett's teasing tone made him smile with ease. He quickly obliged and stepped forward.

The first course was nice and easy with its flat surface and unobstructed pathway. He placed his ball on the ground, lined up his putter, and swung. The bright green golf ball rolled its way over six feet of red and blue synthetic turf until it fell into the hole at the end. Devin pumped his fist in a sign of victory.

"Nice!" she exclaimed. "My turn now!"

"Hold on, I get to ask you a question first."

"I was hoping you'd forgotten in your old age," she teased. "Go on, let's get it over with."

He had one question he desperately wanted Scarlett to answer, but he decided to start off slow. There was no need to rush as he was sure he'd have plenty of opportunities with 32 holes ahead of them. "I want to know why you stayed up so late last night. What did you do that was worth losing sleep over?"

"Oh, that. I have a side job that I mostly do for fun. I needed to meet a deadline today, that's why I was up late."

"Interesting. What kind of side job?"

"Only one question per hole! It's my turn." Scarlett took her time situating the ball on the turf before giving it a light swing. The ball started off with a steady momentum, then gradually ran out of steam as it traveled along the course. When it stopped just short of the hole, Scarlett groaned. "No! No no no. Don't stop, you're almost there! You can do it!"

The sight of a grown woman cheering on a golf ball was one of the most ridiculous yet endearing things Devin had ever witnessed. "I've never seen anyone yell at a golf ball before."

"It just needs a little encouragement. It's literally at the edge of the hole!"

"Just give it a tap. That's all it needs to go in."

"But that won't be a hole in one and I won't be able to ask you a question!" With her hands on her hips, she glanced around the course. "Where's the wind when you need it?"

"And you said I was competitive." Devin couldn't stop grinning, which only served to add fuel to Scarlett's fire. Her cheeks darkened to a rosy pink color that made her look even more beautiful. As much as he enjoyed seeing her pout, he didn't want to frustrate her longer than necessary. "How about this? You can ask me a question, but I get to ask you another one."

"I don't need any special favors, Devin. Just give me a few minutes. I'm sure there will be a gust blowing by soon."

"You may not need any favors, but I do. I'd like to finish the rest of this course before I really become an old grandpa."

"Ha ha," she deadpanned. "All right, we'll go with your plan. But just so we're clear, this is not me giving up. I'm moving on so we'll have enough time to get through the rest of the course, which will give you more time to practice coming up with questions for your real date."

"I appreciate you looking out for me," he drawled with obvious sarcasm. "Go on. What's your question?"

"It's what I wanted to know before. How did you teach yourself to read music?"

"I didn't. I learned by listening. My mom was a concert pianist before she got married. I used to listen to her play for hours at a time and I did my best to copy what she did. Sometimes she'd play the left hand while I played the right. It didn't matter what piece we played as long as we played together." He ran a hand through his hair, surprised at how much he'd shared. "I haven't talked about her with anyone in a long time. It feels nice to be able to."

To his surprise, she stepped closer and placed a hand on his arm. Her sweet floral scent matched the pleasant smile curving her lips. "I'm really glad you shared that with me. Your mom sounds like an amazing person."

"She was. She was the best."

"I'm sure she's proud of the man you've become."

"I don't know about that."

"You should really give yourself more credit." Scarlett gave his arm a squeeze. The gesture was like that of a friend, full of grace. She then nudged him playfully. "All right, what else do you want to ask me?"

Devin's shoulders relaxed as an unexplainable peace filled him. It was in this instant that his world shifted on its axis. He knew with great clarity that he could fall for this woman, and there would be no turning back. Scarlett was accepting, patient, and kind. She didn't pry and try to push him to say more. Her emerald-green eyes held a depth of understanding few people their age, or even older, had. She was something else. Could it be that he had found a true match in his matchmaker?

If so, there was no time to waste.

"I want to know what you want."

She blinked in surprise. "What I want? What do you mean? There's a lot of things that I'd like. Matching shoes, for one thing. To get a hole in one sometime today. To go home and take a nap later—that would be a bonus."

"I want to know what you want for your life."

"Oh." Her voice grew soft. "I don't think anyone's ever asked me that before."

"But you've certainly thought about it, haven't you?"

"I have. That dream I told you about before—getting married and raising a family—that was what I wanted for a long time. But I've learned that you don't always get what you want, and I've accepted that. I know I'm still lovable in God's eyes, and maybe I'll meet the right guy one day, or maybe I won't. Whatever happens though, I want to live my life with no regrets and make the most of every day."

He nodded. "You want a simple but meaningful life."

"I suppose so. You're probably thinking that I should dream bigger. All my sisters have done incredible things with their life. It wasn't for lack of trying on my part; I just don't have the same talents and gifts as they do. It's okay. I try not to compare, but I don't always succeed. Anyway, that was more information than you wanted to know. Should we go on to the next hole?"

Devin moved in front of her before she could take a step. Reaching out, he brushed a lock of hair from her forehead and let his hand linger on her warm cheek. The sadness in her eyes tore him up, especially when she tried so hard to smile through it. He couldn't let her go on believing that she wasn't good enough. "You shouldn't compare yourself to anyone else. You're perfect, just the way you are."

"Nice job. I know you're practicing rule number five, but I'm not your real date." She gave his chest a pat. "Save your compliments for later, Devin."

He grabbed her hand and held it tight in his. "I may be good at many things, but keeping my opinions to myself isn't one of them. I'm not practicing, Scarlett."

Confusion flickered in her eyes as she swallowed hard. "What are you doing then?"

His gaze lowered to her lips as he realized exactly what he wanted to do. He wanted to kiss his matchmaker.

CHAPTER 14
Scarlett

Was Devin going to kiss her?

The thought crossed Scarlett's mind like a ray of sunshine breaking through a dark sky. She felt the warmth of his words like a balm to her soul. She knew she was perfect the way she was—perfectly loved and accepted by God. This was a truth she reminded herself of every day, but to have it spoken out loud made it all the more tangible. And to imagine that this wonderful man would think so much of her—she was about ready to kiss him first herself!

If only that didn't go against everything she stood for as a matchmaker.

Scarlett didn't even want to imagine what her Nanna would think about her now! She was inches away from crossing a line she'd never be able to come back from. Where was her head, and why couldn't her heartbeat stop racing? This was the man who had frustrated her with his big ego and snarky comments just a few days ago. Yet all she could feel for him in this moment was a deep affection.

What did all this mean?

"If you're not practicing, Devin," she asked again, "what are you doing?"

"I—"

"Red?" a man called out from behind them, "is that you?"

A chill ran down Scarlett's spine to hear that familiar voice from her past. She spun around and came face to face with a raven-haired man dressed in designer clothes. His brown eyes looked her up and down, making her insides twist with discomfort. What was her ex doing here? "Conrad, hi! Long time no see."

"It has been a long time, but I remembered that dress of yours. You haven't changed at all, Red. You're still as gorgeous as ever."

Scarlett squirmed under his attentive gaze. Her ex had always been a charmer, and even more so after he got into politics. But charisma and authenticity had a hard time coexisting in his world. She honestly didn't know how she had managed to stay in his life for as long as she had either. Everything about Conrad, from his boisterous voice to his flashy jewelry, called out for attention. He was all about putting on a show, one that seemed to have Devin intrigued by the intense look in his eyes.

Stepping in between her and Conrad, Devin offered his hand. "I'm Devin. Who might you be?"

"I'm Congressman Conrad Gray, proud representative of the 14th district of California. Also known as Red's ex-fiancé. She and I go way back. Don't we, darling?"

"Way, way back, thank the Lord," Scarlett agreed under her breath. In response to Conrad, she squeezed out a tense smile. "It feels like a lifetime ago. What brings you here? Miniature golf was never your thing."

"I'm here with the wife and kids." He pointed to a fashionably dressed woman with two small children who were lined up to play the beginner's course. "Vicky's just made partner at her law firm and our twin boys are at the top of their preschool class. What about you? Have you made something of yourself yet?"

The condescension coating his words reminded her so much

of his mother's last statement to her. *You're not the girl our Conny needs. Why don't you go make something of yourself first?* Scarlett took a shaky breath, determined not to give in to self-pity. She knew her worth in the Lord, but sometimes fear and doubt still crept into the corners of her mind. This chance meeting, however, could be the perfect opportunity to look her insecurity in the eye and finally stand up for herself.

Or at least go down trying.

"I'm doing well, and I'm content with where I am in life. That's all that matters to me."

Conrad snickered as he puffed out his chest. "In other words, you never made it as an actress and you're still single. If you had stayed with me, you would've gotten somewhere by now."

Scarlett winced. His words made her more sad than hurt. This wasn't the man she'd known a decade ago. Any pity she'd felt for herself was now directed at Conrad. Relief filled her to know she had made the right decision when she'd ended their relationship. She could confidently tell him that now.

Before she could open her mouth to reply, she felt Devin's arm around her shoulders, pulling her close. Too surprised to speak, she could only focus on the warmth and security his embrace offered. He smelled amazing, too—fresh and musky with a hint of spice. When she glanced up into his blue eyes, she saw the steadiness and strength she felt in his arms. The look he gave her said one thing—trust me. And for some unknown reason, she did.

"That's where you're wrong, Congressman," Devin boldly remarked. "If Scarlett had stayed with you, she would never have known true happiness, the kind that she's found with me. Not because she needs to make something of herself to be loved, but because I'm smart enough to see her worth and to know how to treat her as the amazing woman that she is and always has been. I'm very glad you and I met, so I now know what kind of man you are and whom I won't be voting for in the next election."

Conrad raised his chin in defiance. "As if I need your measly little vote to win. Who do you think you are?"

"You may not know me, but my grandfather Ezra Kendall knew your family well. I believe your father owes him a debt of gratitude for saving his life."

Conrad's eyes bulged with a mixture of shock and irritation. "You've got to be kidding me. Of all the people in the world? How'd the two of you end up together?"

"Scarlett's the one who found me and took a chance on me, and I'm grateful she did. Now if you'll excuse us, we have an important game to get back to."

Devin guided Scarlett on to the next hole as she stumbled along in disbelief. Did she just witness Devin put her ex in his place? Conrad had to be beside himself! She snuck a look over her shoulder and nearly burst out laughing. The bewilderment on his face was pure comedic gold.

"I kind of feel bad for him," she whispered to Devin. "I've never seen Conrad speechless before! What in the world was that all about? How did your grandfather save his dad's life?"

"His dad worked for my grandfather when he was younger. The story goes that one time when he got a DUI and was thrown into jail, Grandad was the one who bailed him out. Grandad also knew the cop who pulled him over and convinced him to have the case dismissed before it went to court. He then invited him to church and took him under his wing. Grandad didn't save his life in the literal sense, but he helped give him a chance to start over. That's the kind of guy my grandfather was—he cared about his employees and treated them like family."

"That's incredible. I wish I'd had the chance to meet him."

"He would've liked you. He liked people who spoke their minds. I wish he'd had the chance to meet you, too."

Their steps slowed to a stop, and Scarlett turned toward Devin. He still had his arm around her, so they were now mere inches apart. Once again, her senses picked up on how good he smelled and how safe she felt to be near him. All her questions from earlier, along with their mixed emotions, returned in full force. He'd been a heartbeat from kissing her before, or so she'd thought. Did he still want to? Because after the way he'd stood up for her in front of her ex, she could only assume he felt something for her, too.

Unless it had been part of the ruse?

There was only one way to find out.

"Thank you for helping me out just now. For the record, I was about to tell him off myself, but I appreciate you stepping in when you did." Her tone softened as she added, "You said some really nice things about me and I know it was part of the act, but it was still nice to hear."

"I have no doubt you would have held your ground with him. You have no problem putting me in my place when I need it." The corners of his eyes crinkled as he grinned. "You do that well, maybe too well."

"I do, don't I?"

His smile gave way to a more serious demeanor as he tipped her chin up. "But I couldn't stand by and do nothing while he spewed that nonsense about you. I would never let anyone mistreat the woman I love."

Scarlett's stomach dipped to hear the words *the woman I love*. She assumed though that he meant it in the context of the role he'd been playing as her pretend boyfriend. There was no way he'd feel that way about her. They'd only just met, and love was a big word. The only man who had ever told her he loved her was the one who'd chosen his career over her. Devin had to be speaking figuratively.

She offered him a pleased smile. "I'm impressed, Devin. You're really putting your all into this lesson. By the time your date shows up, you're going to be more than ready. Our practicing has really paid off."

"Like I told you before—I'm not practicing. I meant every.

Single. Word." The low timbre of his voice resonated as he emphasized each syllable. "You are amazing and perfect and everything that I'm looking for. You were wrong when you said I wouldn't get along with a strong, independent woman because that's who you are. You're exactly what I need, Scarlett. You're the woman I want to be with."

Scarlett swallowed hard. This couldn't be real, could it? Devin professing his love for her in the middle of a miniature golf course after they'd just bumped into her ex and before he was supposed to go on a date with a woman she'd matched him with—none of it made sense. But she couldn't deny the desire in his eyes nor the joy welling up in her heart. All she wanted was to kiss Devin and show him how much she wanted to be with him, too.

So, she did.

Grabbing a handful of his shirt, she leaned in until her mouth found his. The moment their lips met, Devin's arm snaked around her waist, and he pulled her flush against himself. He didn't waste a second as he kissed her back, slowly and fully, savoring every touch and taste she offered. Scarlett felt her knees go weak as her head spun with anticipation. She never would have imagined Devin could be so passionate yet tender. There was still much to discover about this man who had captured her heart and mind. He was a better man than she could have asked for or deserved. And to be held and kissed like this—Scarlett had never felt so loved. Devin accepted her for who she was and that meant everything to her.

She would have gone on kissing him as long as possible if it weren't for the sudden sound of a child's voice beside them.

"Are you guys gonna play or are you gonna keep on kissing? 'Cause you've been kissing for a really long time."

Scarlett reluctantly broke off the kiss to find a little boy not older than five or six staring up at them. "You're right, we have been kissing for a long time, haven't we?"

"Not long enough," Devin grumbled, still holding her tight.

"But I suppose we could take our kissing somewhere more private."

"I like the way you think."

His blue eyes sparkled in amusement. "Does that mean you like me for more than my looks? I seem to recall you saying I'm hot."

"How is your memory so good, Grandpa?" She shot him a teasing grin before grabbing his hand. As she led him off the course, she called out to the boy, "It's all yours, young man. Have fun!"

"Yes, finally!"

The boy sent them off with an eager wave that had them both laughing. They quickly dropped off the golfing equipment they'd rented, then headed through the arcade to the exit.

Scarlett marveled at how natural it felt to hold Devin's hand. It was so natural that she forgot the reason why they were at the golf course in the first place—until she spotted Devin's date, Cora, standing at the entrance. She tried to pull away before the other woman saw them together, but it was too late.

"What is going on here, Ms. Hayes?" Cora demanded as she marched over. "Why in the world are you holding my date's hand?"

"I-it's not what you think," Scarlett began, her voice strained. Panic coursed through her as she realized there was no easy explanation. "I mean, it kind of is, but I didn't mean for this to happen."

Devin stepped forward. "I can explain—"

"Save your breath," Cora huffed. "The Better Business Bureau's going to be getting an earful from me about your so-called matchmaking services."

Without another word, she stormed off, leaving Scarlett to wonder how she'd ever come back from such a horrible mistake.

CHAPTER 15
Devin

Devin hadn't seen or heard from Scarlett in two days. After their run-in with Cora at the miniature golf course, she'd told him she needed to do damage control. He had offered to help, but she'd said it was a mess that she'd gotten herself into and had to get herself out of.

A mess.

That's what Scarlett called the start of their relationship. For him, it was anything but messy. Owning up to his feelings for her and confessing them out loud made perfect sense to him. Now that he had Scarlett in his life, he couldn't imagine a world without her in it. And three days away from the woman he loved was three days too many.

Immediately, after he left the office on Tuesday night, he got into his car and dialed his sister's number.

"Bekah, I need Scarlett's address," he requested as soon as she answered. "Do you have it?"

"I do, but why don't you ask her for it? And why are you going over to see her? Is she okay? I texted her yesterday, but all she said was that she needed prayer. What's going on?"

Loosening his tie, Devin held back his impatience. He didn't have time to play 20 questions, but he also didn't want to take his frustrations out on Bekah. "I'll tell you everything later. For now, my priority is to see Scarlett. Will you please give me her address?"

"Okay, I'll text it to you, but can you tell her to give me a call? I'm worried about her."

"You and me both," he murmured under his breath. "Thanks, sis. I'll tell her to call you."

Thirty minutes and ten miles of traffic later, he reached her apartment building in South San Jose. The sun was upon the horizon when he jogged upstairs to the second floor. After knocking loudly on the door, he leaned against the frame and waited. It felt like an eternity before it opened.

"Oh, it's you!" The redhead from Scarlett's office greeted him with a disapproving frown. "It's about time you showed up! What took you so long?"

"Sorry, what? Were you expecting me?" He ran a hand through his hair, confused. If his memory served him correctly, this woman was Emerald, one of Scarlett's sisters. "Is Scarlett here?"

"She's here. She's been holed up in her room since the news broke. Come on in." Sighing, Emerald gestured for him to follow. As she led him through a small living room with yellow painted walls and a dark gray couch, she talked to Devin over her shoulder. "I told her to call you, but she didn't want to bother you. But I said you, as her boyfriend, would want to know how she's doing and what you can do to help. Am I right?"

"Right," Devin agreed, too surprised to say more. Those words, *her boyfriend*, had a nice ring to them. He'd been called many titles in his life—son, brother, grandson, and CEO—but never a boyfriend. This was one role he looked forward to filling.

When they stopped at the end of the hall, Emerald turned to him with a stern expression. "I know you're a big shot CEO and you're not used to taking orders from other people, but this is my baby sister we're talking about, Mr. Kendall. If you hurt Scarlett in any way, you're going to have me *and* our two older sisters on your case. Do I make myself clear?"

He understood and respected the threats of an older sibling. Without any hesitation, he stated, "Crystal. I would never do anything to hurt Scarlett. You have my word."

"Good!" She knocked on Scarlett's door and called out, "Hey, Red, are you decent? Your honey's here to see you."

"Yes, come in."

Emerald stepped aside to allow Devin to enter. "You two have fun, but not too much fun, you hear? I'm going out for a bit. Be back later."

Devin's eyes adjusted to the dim lighting before he spotted Scarlett sprawled out on a full-size bed in the middle of the room. With her floral comforter pulled up to her nose, only her large green eyes were on display behind a pair of glasses. One of her hands appeared and waved him over.

He took a seat on the edge of her bed. "Why haven't you been answering my calls or texts?" he demanded. Seeing her wince, he quickly softened his tone. "I've been worried about you. Bekah has been, too."

"I know. I'm sorry for making you guys worry. I just haven't been in the mood to talk to anyone." She stared up at the ceiling and sighed. "Everything's been so crazy since that article came out in the paper yesterday."

"What article?"

"You didn't hear? It was titled 'Reservations Canceled for Party of Two.' Cora just so happens to be good friends with one of the editors at The Mercury News. Now the whole Silicon Valley knows what happened on Saturday. It wouldn't be so bad if it just affected me, but it's affecting our business. Some of our clients are backing out and asking for a refund. And there are others coming out of the woodwork claiming that I flirted with their dates and that's why their matches didn't work out. We've gotten more one-star reviews in the last twenty-four hours than the last twenty-four years! I hate that my family has to suffer for a mistake I made. I'm not calling us a mistake," she quickly added as she sat up. "I just wish I had handled things differently. You understand, don't you? Please don't be mad at me, too."

"I'm not mad at you." How could he be, especially when she was wearing those ridiculous frog PJs again. She had no idea how adorable she looked right now. "I could never be mad at you."

"You sure about that?" Her brows furrowed until a line formed between them. "I seem to recall you being mad at me after your date with Moira went south."

"I was more frustrated than anything." He took ahold of her hands and held them between his. "I'm making a new rule. From this point forward, there will be no more talk about my dates with other women. The only woman I'm interested in dating is you."

Scarlett smiled genuinely for the first time since he'd arrived. "I'm really happy to hear that 'cause you're kind of the only good thing to come out of all of this."

"Kind of? I seem to recall it was you who kissed me first. And you seemed to really enjoy it."

She wrinkled her nose in chagrin. "It was all your fault, you know. You just had to pour your heart out to me and make me feel so special. My love language happens to be words of affirmation."

"Is it? Good to know."

"What's yours? Let me guess—" She paused to think. "Acts of service?"

"Exactly." He nodded, impressed that she could tell that much about him. "I know people talk about how it's the thought that counts, but since no one has the ability to read minds, we can only rely on actions."

"That's why they also say actions speak louder than words. They're probably not the same people though who say it's the thought that counts."

"Likely not." He brushed a lock of hair from her face and

tucked it behind her ear. His fingers lingered on her cheek, enjoying the intimacy of this small gesture. He and Scarlett had become so comfortable with one another in such a short period of time, and all he longed for now was to be closer to her. Tilting her chin up, he murmured, "I appreciate acts of service, but I'm not opposed to physical touch."

Her gaze dropped to his mouth. "Are you saying you wouldn't mind if I kissed you again?"

"I'm saying I would mind if you didn't—"

The sentence was barely out of his mouth before Scarlett wrapped her arms around his neck. She teased him with a soft peck at first, leaving him wanting more, then deepened the kiss to allow him to experience her fully. It was only their second kiss, but he was already familiar with everything Scarlett offered him—her unique taste and scent and sounds. The knowledge that a woman so kind, giving, and loving would agree to be his filled him with more happiness than he'd felt in a long time. His heart drummed in his chest as she leaned in close, sending a surge of need through his body. Being alone with her in this room was more than he could handle. Reluctantly, he broke off the kiss and sat back to put some distance between them.

"Now I'm the one enjoying the kiss a little too much," he joked, trying to catch his breath. The emotions brimming in his heart were ones he'd never experienced before. How could he feel so much for Scarlett already? He'd do anything to care for her and protect her. The thought made him all the more aware of how much was at stake. He clenched his hands at the realization that he'd already failed to protect her from the fallout of Saturday's situation.

"Are you okay?" Scarlett took his hand and gave it a squeeze. "You got quiet all of a sudden. What are you thinking about?"

"I'm going to figure out a way to clean up this mess. Those accusations being thrown out there about you—they're false and you shouldn't have to deal with them. This is grounds for a libel lawsuit. I'll make things right for you, Scarlett, I promise."

"Whoa, slow your roll, Mr. CEO," she exclaimed. "I don't want to sue anyone. I'm hoping this news will die down in a few days when the next piece of gossip comes in. And anyway, not everything they said is untrue. I did break the cardinal rule of matchmaking, which is to never get involved with a client. I made the choice to cross the line. I just never imagined the outcome would be so public. But these are my consequences, and I accept them."

"You're just going to give up like that?"

"I'm not giving up. I'm still praying. I have faith that God will work things out for me and the business. He'll let me know what I need to do."

"You're going to pray and wait?" He ran a hand down his face. The sarcasm coating his words was more than he'd wanted to show, but it was too late to take it back. He might as well be up front with Scarlett about his faith, or lack of it. "That's your game plan?"

"Yes. That's what I usually do. Don't you ask God for help?"

"To be honest, not anymore. I've had to learn to solve my own problems. He has other, more important things to deal with."

"That's not true. God cares about everything that you care about. You matter to Him, Devin." Frowning, she pulled him into a tight embrace. "I can't believe you'd think otherwise. If He loved you enough to pay for your sins through Jesus' death on the cross, don't you think He'd want to listen to your prayers and answer them, too?"

Devin almost laughed to hear the worry in her sweet voice. "I thought I was the one comforting you, not the other way around. I appreciate your concern, but I'm fine. It's you that I'm worried about."

She drew back to look him in the eyes. Her gaze didn't waver for one moment as she said, "If you're worried about me, then promise you'll pray for me. That's the best thing you can do."

Since he truly loved Scarlett, he nodded in agreement. But just because he agreed didn't mean he couldn't also do something to help the situation. A plan began forming in his mind as to how to save Scarlett's reputation and her family business.

CHAPTER 16
Scarlett

When Scarlett walked into the office on Friday morning with Emerald by her side, she hung her head in shame. After staying home the past couple of days, she'd finally gotten the courage to come in. Showing up was the easy part; getting back into Amber's and Capri's good graces was an entirely different matter.

She straightened her back to stand tall in her heels. She'd worn her favorite hot pink power suit in the hopes of appearing as put together as possible. If she looked professional, maybe her sisters would conveniently forget that she'd done the most unprofessional thing.

If not, she would most certainly need divine intervention.

"Pray for me, Em," she whispered out of the corner of her mouth.

"Will do! You've got this, Red!" Emerald murmured before slipping away down the hall to her office.

Unfortunately, the moment Scarlett saw her older sisters' stern faces, she wanted to crawl back to bed and hide beneath the covers. She'd only gotten on their bad side a handful of times, and those instances had all been during their childhood when she hadn't known better. This time, she had no excuse. Taking a deep breath, she squeezed out the brightest, most apologetic smile. At least she'd been smart enough to bring a peace offering.

"Good morning, sweet sisters of mine!" She handed each one of them a cup. "One Caramel Macchiato for you, Amber, and a Flat White for you, Capri."

Amber furrowed her brows. "If you're trying to appease us, caffeine is a good way to start."

"A very good way," Capri chimed in. Her expression softened as she took a sip, then sighed happily. "All right, I forgive you."

"Already, Capri?" chided Amber in a hushed voice. "We're supposed to drag this out at least an hour longer, remember?"

"I know, but it's hard to stay mad at Red when she's giving you those puppy dog eyes. Just look at her. That's how she always got her way when we were kids."

Scarlett exaggerated her pout and brought her palms together in a begging pose. "I'm really, really sorry for creating such a mess, guys. I never meant to fall for my client. I don't even know how it happened. I couldn't stand Devin a week ago, and now I can't imagine my life without him. None of it makes sense, but in a strange way, it all makes sense. Am I even making sense right now?"

"Oh goodness, Emerald was right," Amber lamented, "you do have it bad."

Capri nodded. "So bad. How well do you know this guy, Red? Is Devin as amazing as you think he is, or have you been blinded by his good looks?"

"I'm not that shallow! I love his mind and his heart, too." Scarlett leaned against the reception desk as she recalled how sweet he'd been when he'd visited her a few days ago. He'd been so concerned for her well-being and had tried his best to comfort her. The memory of their kiss replayed in her mind, bringing a smile to her face. "Okay, I do have it bad, but in a good way. Devin is everything I want in a man, and I couldn't be happier."

Amber winced as she placed a hand on her hip. "I hate to burst your rose-colored bubble, but that's what you said about Conrad when you first got together, and it took you four years to see his true colors. I don't want to see you waste another four years of your life on a guy who's not who he says he is. You should get to know him better before deciding to become Mrs.—what's his last name?"

"Kendall," Capri filled in for her. "Scarlett Kendall. Or maybe Scarlett Hayes Kendall? I'd go with the second one."

"I'm not marrying him anytime soon, guys! We just started dating." Scarlett pursed her lips as she regarded her oldest sister. Amber didn't mince words, especially when it came to her opinions about mistakes Scarlett had made in the past. Of course, Amber meant well, but it still stung to not have her approval, especially about a matter as important as this one. "I understand your concern, Amber, but Devin is nothing like Conrad. And I'm a lot smarter than I was when I was in college."

"I sure hope so. But I'd still like to meet him. When's the soonest you can bring him around?"

"You already met him when he came in last week."

Capri chuckled. "What Amber's saying is that she wants to do some barbequing, as in grill him."

"Yes, I want to meet and grill this guy who's cost our family so much business this past week," Amber stated with a tone devoid of any humor.

"It wasn't all Devin's doing," Scarlett insisted, "I had a part in it, too. I was the one who kissed him first at Golfland."

"Spare me the details, Scarlett. The two of you must have already started to have feelings before that day. I don't understand why he'd still agree to go on the date you had arranged for him or why you'd still agree to matchmake for him. This mess could have been prevented if you had just talked things out."

"I think that's kinda what happened when you guys kissed,

right?" Capri asked Scarlett, her tone rhetorical. "Show her some grace, Amber. Red didn't mean to fall for Devin."

"That would be a lot easier to do if we didn't have bills to pay."

Scarlett's shoulders sagged with regret. Their matchmaking business had already suffered a setback a few years ago when online dating apps started to get popular. Since then, Amber had worked hard to re-strategize their marketing to bring in more clients. All Scarlett had done was sabotage things. *What do I do, Lord?* If she ever needed wisdom, it was now.

"I'll find a way to fix this, guys, I promise." An idea came to her. "What if we offer a special deal for the holidays? This is around the time when people start looking for a date to bring to their company parties and family gatherings. I'll put an ad together offering new clients fifteen percent off and get it posted on social media today. I'm sure it'll bring in tons of business!"

Amber and Capri exchanged wary looks that had Scarlett throwing her hands up in the air. Frustration tightened her shoulders as her patience ran out. "I know you guys usually have all the great ideas, but that doesn't mean I can't come up with one, too. You're not even giving it a chance."

"It's not that we don't think it's a good idea," Capri reassured her. "The problem is that if it does bring in more clients, we're not going to be able to handle them all."

"What do you mean? There's four of us. We can totally take on a couple more clients each."

Amber blew out a long breath. "We've already had to take on your workload this week, so that's three more cases for each of us. We're spread thin as it is."

"I know, but I'm here now. I'll be taking those clients back from you guys."

"I wish it were that simple." Capri walked over and placed her arm around Scarlett's shoulders. "The thing is, all your clients but one have expressed reservations about having you as their matchmaker. They said they'd rather work with someone else, so we had to follow through on their requests."

"You guys did what?"

"I'm sorry, Red. Under the circumstances, we thought it was the right thing to do."

"I can't believe it." Scarlett shook free of Capri's arm as disappointment twisted her insides. "Did you guys explain to them what happened? Did you even try to stand up for me?"

"Of course, we did," Amber stated matter-of-factly, "you're our baby sister. We've stood up for you your whole life. We've always cleaned up your messes. But this is one mess that's beyond our control. We're doing what we have to do to keep the business running."

Scarlett's throat burned and tears blurred her vision. *We've always cleaned up your messes.* Is that what her sisters thought about her—that she was only good at making mistakes that they had to fix? "I'm sorry I've made life so hard for you guys. But don't worry, you won't have to clean up my messes anymore. I quit."

She covered her mouth to stop herself from sobbing out loud, then quickly turned and fled the office.

CHAPTER 17
Devin

Devin ran through the doors of his home and straight into Bekah, nearly knocking her over. His heart had been racing ever since his sister called him at work, urging him to come home. "Where's Scarlett?"

"She's in the kitchen." Bekah picked up her purse that had fallen off her shoulder when Devin had bumped into her. "Thanks for coming, Dev. I didn't want to leave her alone, but I have to get to class. You're on boyfriend duty now!"

"Boyfriend duty?" he muttered as he watched his sister leave without a backward glance. He ran a hand down his face and released a heavy breath, unsure of what those words entailed. All he'd heard from Bekah was that Scarlett had quit her job and was having an emotional meltdown. Nothing on his resume qualified him to handle something like this, but for Scarlett's sake, he'd tackle the issue head-on and resolve it for her.

He marched over to the kitchen, ready to problem-solve, when he came upon a scene that had him at a loss for words. There stood Scarlett wearing a bright pink suit with her hair tied up in a bun on the top of her head. A layer of flour covered the countertop where she was kneading a large ball of dough. A baking tray full of cookies sat on her right and a pan of brownies on her left. The sweet smell of sugar and chocolate hung in the air, welcoming him inside, yet his feet remained still as he lingered in the doorway. This was not the state he'd expected to find Scarlett in. He'd left his busy workday for this?

"Hey, what's going on?" Taking tentative steps, he walked over to Scarlett. "Is everything okay?"

"Devin!" She dropped the dough and jumped into his arms. She clung to him and started crying. "No, everything's not okay. My sisters said I'm a burden, so I told them I was quitting. Now they probably think I'm abandoning them when the business is in trouble, but I don't know how else to help. I'd just make things worse by staying. I don't know what to do. I thought I had faith that God was going to work everything out, but I don't know anymore. Why can't I do anything right?"

There was the meltdown he'd been warned about. He pulled back to assess her condition. With her red-rimmed eyes and pink nose, she looked quite helpless but still beautiful. He wiped away some traces of flour on her cheeks, then held her gaze without blinking. This wasn't anything some good old common sense couldn't fix.

"I know things may seem bad now, but there's a solution for every problem. Nothing's too challenging to resolve. Believe me, I've seen plenty of bad scenarios at work. You just need to think through your options. Figure out what your sisters want and what you want and come to a mutual agreement. I'll help you fix this. In fact, I already have something in the works that will redeem the business's reputation."

Scarlett stared up at him, a mixture of sadness and disappointment reflected in her eyes. A wistful smile crossed her lips when she replied, "I love that you dropped everything to come see me and that you feel so passionately about helping, but I'm not a problem to fix, Devin."

"I didn't call you the problem. The problem is with the

rumors going around about your family's business, and whatever is happening between you and your sisters is a simple misunderstanding. I can fix—"

She cut him off with a shake of her head. "I know you can probably fix just about anything, but right now all I want is for you to listen and hold me and pray for me." She ended her sentence with a questioning tone, as if she were unsure how he'd take her request. Her gaze dropped when he didn't reply. "Or you can help me knead this dough. If you haven't noticed, I like to bake when I'm upset. It gives me time to think and vent to God about what's going on. And beating dough up is a good way to get my emotions out. You should try it."

Devin watched helplessly as she turned toward the counter. Everything she asked of him was in opposition to what he was used to doing. His body itched to move and react, but all she wanted was for him to be still. He was reminded of a Bible verse his grandfather used to have hanging up in his office. *Be still, and know that I am God.* Devin gritted his teeth and clenched his hands. He had never been good with inaction.

As simple as Scarlett's request seemed on the surface, it would take every ounce of self-control within him to follow through. Sure, listening and holding her would be easy—if he didn't also have to hold his tongue and keep his opinions and suggestions to himself. Harder still would be the act of prayer because that would mean he'd have to ask God for help. In asking, he would need to admit that he didn't have all the answers and would have to wait on the Lord for a solution.

That was precisely why he didn't pray.

But Scarlett had asked him to. She was everything he didn't want to be—vulnerable and dependent—yet she was so much braver than he could ever profess to be. Her intentions were pure and genuine, without any pretenses. She made him long for more than the structured and safe world that he had built for himself.

Could he put enough trust in God to let go of his need for control?

He would try.

Devin stepped up behind Scarlett and wrapped his arms around her. She stilled and leaned into his embrace with a soft sigh. Holding her tight, he placed a gentle kiss on the top of her head. Chalky powder dusted his lips from the flour on her hair, but he paid no heed to it. All he wanted was to show Scarlett how much he loved her.

"Asking for help isn't something I'm good at, but I'm willing to try."

She placed her hands over his and nodded. "Thank you."

He closed his eyes and prayed, "God, I know You are more than capable of helping Scarlett. I ask that You make a way for her out of this situation and help her to work things out with her sisters. In Jesus' name, amen."

Scarlett spun around in his arms until they were face to face. She cupped his cheeks, then dusted off the traces of flour on his skin and regarded him with a grateful smile. "Thank you, Devin. That meant more to me than you know."

His throat tightened, making it hard to speak. "You mean more to me than you know. Thank you for being patient with me."

"Thank you for being patient with me. I know I'm probably a lot more than you expected or know what to do with. My Nanna used to say I wore my heart on both sleeves and pant legs. I guess I just feel a lot, and it sometimes leaks out. Sorry for dumping it all on you."

"You don't need to apologize. I like that about you."

"You're not just saying that because you're trying to be a good boyfriend, are you?"

"Of course not. Wait, what do you mean trying? Aren't I one already?" he added with a playful smirk.

"You are! I can't believe you came home in the middle of a workday. I told Bekah not to call you."

"I'm glad she did. But next time, I expect you to call me first. You shouldn't go through these things alone. I can help, and by that, I mean I can listen and hold you and pray for you. You just let me know when you need me, and I'll do my best to be there."

"You learn fast, Mr. CEO. Thank you," she murmured before pressing her mouth to his.

Surprised, he held onto the countertop as she relayed the gratitude of her words in this tangible way. She pulled him closer, her soft curves melding with the hard planes of his body. Heat rushed through his body with every touch. How could every kiss with Scarlett feel like a new and better experience? He would never grow tired of this intimate act of giving and receiving. There was so much more he desired to learn about her, not only in the physical sense but intellectually and emotionally as well. God willing, he would very much like to live out the rest of his days falling more and more in love with Scarlett Hayes.

Ding!

His phone sounded, reminding him of a meeting on his calendar. He reluctantly broke off their kiss to silence the alarm.

"Do you have to go?" Scarlett asked softly as she smoothed down the front of his shirt. "We've hardly seen each other all week."

"I know. Things have been hectic with this company acquisition that we've been working on. My schedule should be better after the deal closes next month. We're aiming to wrap it up before the holidays."

She nodded, focusing her attention on the ball of dough on the counter. "I guess I'll go back to baking."

"Or you could go to work. I'm sure your sisters haven't processed your resignation yet." He craned his head to meet her eyes. When she didn't look over, he cradled her chin and tipped it up. "Hey, don't tell me you're giving up so easily. Where's the

Scarlett from last week, the one who didn't hesitate to go toe to toe with me and put me in my place?"

"She was pretty amazing, wasn't she?" A small smile brightened her eyes. "I guess she's in the middle of a mini midlife crisis and trying to decide if matchmaking is really what she wants to do or if she's daring enough to go after her own dream."

"Her—your dream? Is there something else you want to do?"

She began rolling and kneading the dough as she stared off into the distance. With a shrug, she replied, "There is, but it's a long shot. It's more of a hobby right now, but I'd love to do it fulltime if I can."

"Then you should do it. What's stopping you?"

"Lots of things, mostly fear. Fear that I won't be able to pay my bills and fear that my sisters will think it's silly and not a real job. They're all so talented and have done so much with their gifts. I can't even begin to compete with them."

"So don't." He took her by the shoulders. "You're not them. You don't need to do what they've done. You have your own strengths and talents."

"You make it sound so simple. You have no idea what it's like to live in their shadows all your life."

"Need I remind you who my brother is? Try being the identical twin of someone with a song in the Top 40 charts."

"But you could have easily been in the charts, too, with him. You just decided not to be."

"True, but I was never as popular as Jace. He can keep a crowd of thousands entertained for hours at a time, and by the end of the night, they'll still be wanting more. He can make friends with anyone in sight. In case you haven't noticed, I'm not quite as personable."

"You don't say."

Her teasing smile made him chuckle. "My point is, God knew exactly what He was doing when He made you. You're not supposed to be like anyone else; you're you. That's something my grandad used to tell me whenever I compared myself to Jace. You're not your sisters, Scarlett. You just need to be you. Because that's exactly who I fell in love with."

Her green eyes sparkled like emeralds. "Did I hear you say you're in love with me?"

"I am," Devin declared proudly. "Do you have a problem with that?"

"Not at all because I might be in love with you, too."

"Might?"

"I most definitely might."

Those were the words Devin needed to hear to get a plan falling into place. He had begun this matchmaking journey looking for a wife to fulfill a clause, but he had found so much more. Scarlett was more than a solution to a problem; she was the answer to questions he didn't even know he had. His life made sense with her in it. She was his equal match in every possible way and the woman he would gladly lose everything to because with her by his side, he had already won.

It was time to make Scarlett his wife, and he planned on doing so that night.

CHAPTER 18
Scarlett

An evening at the ice-skating rink? Scarlett couldn't think of a more perfect way to spend her first official date with Devin.

"What made you decide to come here?" She gestured at the large white-and-teal building they stood in front of with a sign that read Sharks Ice at Fremont. "I thought you didn't know how to ice-skate."

"I don't," Devin replied as he laced his fingers with hers. "But you made such a big deal about me giving it a try, so I thought, why not?"

"You surprise me, Devin. I didn't think you were that easy to convince. Or maybe my powers of persuasion are really that good."

"Maybe." He shot her a playful wink. "Come on, let's go inside before I change my mind."

Scarlett gladly followed his lead, marveling at how lucky she was to have Devin in her life. Well, luck had nothing to do with it. She was sure this was all part of God's plan, even the mess she'd gotten herself into. Not that God had meant for her to mess up, but He had known all along what would happen and was still gracious and faithful to work everything together for her good. She still didn't know what to do about her job, but she'd decided to set aside the uncertainty for the time being and enjoy her night. For once, her love life was in better shape than her professional life, and she didn't mind it one bit.

She was with the sweetest hunk of a man who was stepping out of his comfort zone for her, and he also truly liked her. No, he loved her. Devin Kendall loved her for who she was. There was no greater feeling than being loved unconditionally.

As they walked through the double doors, a blast of cold air enveloped them, but all Scarlett felt was the warmth of Devin's arm around her shoulders. She snuggled into his side as they headed over to the rental counter. They were the only customers, so it took just a handful of minutes for them to get their skates on and laced. Soon, they were ready for the ice in their matching navy knit hats and scarves that Devin had provided.

"Are you warm enough?" he asked as he pulled the brim of her hat over her ears.

"Very. You thought of everything, Devin. Thank you."

"You're very welcome." He gestured to the empty rink before them. "Ladies first."

As soon as Scarlett stepped onto the ice, she gasped. There in the center of the rink was the outline of a large heart made with pink and red rose petals. White candles decorated its perimeter, their flames flickering like fireflies. Whoever had arranged this had gone all out. It looked like a scene from a movie.

"Do you think it's okay for us to be here?" she called out as she skated a few feet closer for a better look. "It's so beautiful!"

"Of course, it's okay. I reserved the whole place for us."

She spun around, her mouth agape. "You did what? That must have cost a small fortune!"

"Like I said before, money is not an issue for me."

"I guess it isn't." She blinked, still surprised by his gesture. "Did you plan the rose petals and candles, too?"

A flicker of uncertainty passed over his features. "Do you not like it?"

"No, I love it!" She skated back to Devin's side. "It's so sweet and romantic. I'm just surprised. Is this some kind of CEO move that you're trying to impress me with?"

That smirk of his that she had grown to adore made an appearance. "Are you impressed?"

"I am, but you didn't have to go to all this trouble. You should know that I don't need any kind of special treatment." Pointing to her outfit, she remarked, "I'm a jeans and sweatshirt kind of girl. I don't need much."

"I know, but that's not going to stop me from giving you the best. I also prefer not to make a fool of myself in front of a room full of strangers if I can help it." Holding onto the wall for support, Devin took his first steps onto the ice. He moved forward slowly, inch by inch, as if he were walking on stilts. His brows drew together as he winced. "This isn't my finest hour as you can see."

Her heart did a happy little flip as she watched him. If this wasn't a sacrificial act on his part, she didn't know what was. "I disagree. You look pretty hot in those jeans, Devin Kendall. I happen to have a soft spot for guys who go out of their way to make a girl's wish come true."

"You better be talking about one guy, and one guy only." He released his hold on the wall with one hand to point at himself. In doing so, he lost his balance and fell onto the ice with a groan.

Scarlett rushed over and helped him to his feet. "Bend your knees and lean forward a bit. That way you're less likely to get thrown off balance."

"Now you tell me," he muttered through gritted teeth. Red colored his cheeks, likely more from frustration than the cold. "Any other pointers you want to give me before I break my back?"

"You are so dramatic! You're not going to break anything going zero miles an hour," she chided him with a cheeky grin. "If it's any consolation, you did the right thing by landing on your backside. You're less likely to break anything that way, except for your pride."

"Believe me, I'm way ahead of the game on that one."

His droll expression had Scarlett laughing when a young voice suddenly called out to them. "Hey, mister! You look like you need some help!"

A young blonde girl appeared at the entrance to the rink. In her hands was a metal device that Scarlett recognized as a skate trainer. "That's perfect, thanks!"

Stepping onto the ice with her sneakers, the girl walked the apparatus over and unfolded it. With a beaming smile, she offered it to Devin. "Here you go. This will keep you from falling."

"What is this? Some kind of walker?" He eyed it suspiciously, studying the pair of trapezoid frames that were held together by two parallel bars on one side. "I don't need a walker. I can walk fine on my own."

The girl narrowed her blue eyes at Devin. "If you don't want to break anything, you should use the walker."

"Ha! She makes a good point, Devin." Scarlett gave her newfound friend a high five. "What's your name, sweetheart?"

"Ella." She stared up at Devin, recognition lighting up her eyes. "You're my mom's favorite singer!"

He shook his head adamantly. "No, you're thinking of my brother, Jace. I'm Devin."

"Oh."

"Ella, where are you?" a woman called out from a distance. "Come finish your homework!"

"I gotta go! Tell your brother Leah Parker said hi!"

Scarlett watched Ella run off, her ponytail swinging from side to side. "She's cute."

"Humph."

She took one look at Devin's dejected expression and kissed

him on the cheek. "Cheer up, old man! She was just trying to help."

"I'm not upset about the walker. It was the disappointment on her face when she realized I wasn't Jace. You wouldn't believe how many times I got that same reaction when we were younger. For a second, some of those old insecurities came back. Ridiculous, right? Here I am, a grown man and still hung up on things from the past."

"It's not ridiculous, Devin. Just because we look like adults doesn't mean we always feel like one. You're allowed to be vulnerable and insecure."

His eyes clouded with unspoken emotions. "Those words aren't part of my vocabulary. My father made sure of that."

Her heart cracked to hear the hurt in his voice. That explained why Devin was so good at keeping his emotions in check and why he worked so hard at being in control. She ached for the little boy who had to grow up too fast. "You don't have to put up a front with me, Devin. I want to know all of you, especially the parts of you that you don't show the rest of the world. You're safe with me. You know that, right?"

A moment passed before he nodded. A moment in which tears filled his eyes, along with a look of tenderness that stole Scarlett's breath away. In that stillness and quiet, all she could think of was how blessed she was to be able to love Devin in a way that he possibly had never experienced before. *Help me to love this man well, Lord.* That was Scarlett's simple prayer as she wrapped her arms around his waist and held him tight.

She felt Devin's body relax as he rested in her embrace. He kissed the top of her head, then murmured in her ear, "Marry me."

She froze, wondering if she'd heard him wrong. Pulling away to see him, she swallowed hard as she found herself staring at a diamond solitaire ring. It sat in a black velvet box cradled in Devin's palm. Scarlett's gaze flitted from the ring to Devin's hopeful smile and back again as her mind struggled to process the scene.

"Marry me, Scarlett."

"You're asking me to marry you?"

"As of now, I've asked you twice. I don't know how else to make it any clearer. I want to make you my wife."

It dawned on her what the romantic setup on the ice was all about. Devin had arranged this evening at the ice rink to propose to her! She knew he was the kind of man who made things happen, but she'd never expected that to include a marriage proposal on their first date.

"Devin," she began, keeping her tone gentle, "I'm really touched that you did all this for me. I can't even begin to tell you how much it means, not just the roses and the candles and the ring, but how much you've opened up to me. It's a privilege and an honor to have you propose to me. But ..."

His expression sobered and he closed the ring box. "So, it's a no."

"No! I mean, it's not a no, it's more of a not yet." She winced, hating how much she had to be hurting him, especially after she'd claimed to be his safe place. The irony and painfulness of the situation made her throat raw. She couldn't lie to him though. He deserved an explanation. "This is just too much, too soon, Devin. We've only started dating, and my life is kind of up in the air right now with my job situation. I'm not in the right headspace to make a huge decision like this."

"How much time do you need?"

"How much time?" How did she even answer a question like this? Devin was asking her to put a timeline on a relationship that had only begun. It was like a seed that had been laid in fresh soil and still needed to be given time and room to grow. She didn't understand how he could bet so much on something that hadn't proven itself yet. "How are you so sure already? I'm practically a stranger to you. What if I turn out to not be the person you think

I am? What if you decide one day that I'm not the one you want to be with, that I'm not good enough for you? What happens then, Devin? You don't want to be making a decision now that you'll regret a few months or years down the line. You'd only be wasting your time."

A heavy silence fell between them as she avoided his gaze. She could only assume that the truth of her words was weighing heavily on Devin's mind, undoing the impulsiveness that had spurred him to propose. It was too easy to let the haze of hopes and dreams blur reality; she'd made that mistake before.

She finally forced herself to look up. "I'm so sorry, Devin. You and I both need more time."

With a calmness she didn't expect, he simply replied, "I can wait."

CHAPTER 19
Devin

For someone who'd been rejected, Devin felt an odd sense of peace. A week had passed since his failed marriage proposal, yet he was more determined than ever to win Scarlett's trust.

Trust—that's what it all boiled down to.

He understood why Scarlett had said no. She'd been hurt before and sidelined by the ambitions of her ex. No wonder she didn't have faith in their future. Devin had asked her to trust him blindly without any concrete evidence of his commitment to her. It wasn't enough that he'd planned a nice evening out or bought a ring. The real question was if he would stay with her through all the highs and lows of life and if his love for her would ever waver.

The answers were clear to him, and he would do everything in his power to help her see them, too. He would find ways to show Scarlett that he was ready to treasure, honor, and protect her for the rest of his days.

He drummed his fingers on the steering wheel impatiently as he navigated his car through the noontime rush. Taking deep breaths, he reminded himself of what Scarlett had taught him. It was okay to not have all the answers. It was also okay to ask for help. The peace and comfort that flooded his heart made it easier to utter his next words.

"Would You help me, Lord?"

The words rolled off his tongue in a surprisingly effortless way. Devin had come to accept that making Scarlett his wife was an act out of his control. He could not force her to trust him any more than he could cause the sun to rise. But the One who had brought them together and who held their futures in His hands could help guide them along in this journey.

It was merely a matter of time, but unfortunately, time was the one thing he didn't have.

The text he'd gotten from his cousin Nick before he left the office replayed in his mind as he reached his destination.

Hey cuz, get married yet? You've got two months. Good luck!

He had quickly fired off a message to his grandfather's lawyer asking to talk over the weekend. Without the wife he needed to inherit Kendall & Sons, he would have to find another way to ensure his family's company stayed in the right hands.

"Would You help me with this, too, Lord?"

Again, the prayer came from a deep place of need and reliance, one he'd finally allowed himself to tap into after so many years. Scarlett had shown him the strength it took to be vulnerable and the freedom that resulted from letting go. For the first time in a long time, he didn't feel alone. More importantly, he no longer wanted to face the world by himself. He was ready to start trusting and asking for help. And he had Scarlett to thank for this miracle.

Now here he was back at Party of Two to show his gratitude by helping to salvage her family business. Taking a deep breath, he pushed open the door and steeled himself for the enthusiastic welcome he was sure was waiting for him on the other side.

As soon as he stepped into the lobby, however, he was met with absolute silence. Both Amber and Capri stopped talking when they spotted him. The disapproving looks they exchanged made Devin's shoulders tense. Only Emerald offered him a small smile as she walked over to greet him.

"Mr. Kendall, what brings you here today?" She leaned close and added in a soft murmur, "Don't mind them. Their bark is worse than their bite."

He nodded in understanding. "Call me Devin. I'm here on behalf of Scarlett and myself to offer a solution to getting your business back on its feet."

"On behalf of Scarlett?" Amber stomped over, her hands on her hips. "Why isn't she here herself? Does she even care about how we're doing?"

"Of course, she does. She's been beating herself up over what happened." Crossing his arms over his chest, he turned to face Amber. "It's not easy for her to face you, knowing how much she's disappointed you. Scarlett looks up to you—all of you. You three are some of the most important people in her life."

Capri frowned. "Now I feel bad. You were pretty hard on her the other day, Amber. It wasn't like Red fell for Devin on purpose."

"She really didn't," Emerald chimed in, "but can you blame her?"

"Yes, I can, but not only her; him, too." Narrowing her eyes, Amber pinned her gaze on Devin. "When did you start falling for Scarlett? If you knew you were falling for her, why did you still go through with the matchmaking?"

He blinked in surprise. When had he started to fall for Scarlett? It was before that day at the golf course, of course, but if he were to pinpoint the exact moment, he couldn't pick one. "To tell you the truth, I have no idea when it started. She came into my life without warning, like an earthquake that wakes you from a deep sleep. She continued to shake up my world every time I saw her. As hard as I tried not to think about her, I couldn't get her off my mind. I was too stubborn to admit that she'd won me over," he said with a chuckle. "Scarlett is the smartest woman I know, the most generous and compassionate one, too. She not only makes me want to be a better man, she gives me the confidence that I can be. Not because of anything I can do, but because of her faith in me. I would gladly lose to her any day of the week because with her I can only win." He raised his palms in a gesture of surrender. "I take full responsibility for not owning up to my feelings and putting a stop to the matchmaking when I had the chance. If you want to take your anger and frustration out on anyone, take it out on me, but leave Scarlett out of this."

Silence fell over the room as the women stared at Devin. He didn't know what to make of their reaction, but he was ready to stand his ground. Whatever Scarlett's sisters wanted to do to him, he'd take it.

"Are you done?" Amber asked, her tone even.

"That depends. Are you letting Scarlett off the hook?"

She dropped her hands from her hips, taking a neutral stance. With a glance at her sisters, she nodded. "She was never really *on* the hook. I know I said some harsh things—which I do regret—but I also know my sister. She doesn't let just anyone close, especially after what her ex did to her. So, for her to have chosen you, it says a lot about the kind of person you are. And from what you just shared, I think it's safe to say that Scarlett's found someone who's worth this mess she got into. As long as you continue to treat her like a queen, that's all that matters. As for the business, we'll figure it out."

"If that's the only problem, you'll be happy to know that I already have a solution for you," Devin offered with a smile. "I had my PR team do some work. They found some social media influencers who want to partner with you on a couple of giveaway opportunities. And a crew from KRON will be coming out to interview you. They're interested in doing a special piece on matchmaking for the holidays."

"KRON, as in the news station KRON?" Capri shrieked. "We're going to be on TV?"

"That's right. They should be emailing you with details soon. With some good publicity, it shouldn't be long before the public forgets about what happened with Scarlett and me and business picks up again."

"I don't know what to say, Devin." Amber shook her head in disbelief as she held out her hand to him. "I suppose all I can say is welcome to the family! Because if Scarlett doesn't marry you, one of us will!"

"She's kidding, of course," Emerald reassured him. "Thank you, Devin. Not just for saving the business, but thank you for taking care of our sister."

"The pleasure is all mine, truly. I know she wants the best for your business, so if I can help in this small way, I'm more than happy to."

"You know what else you can do to help?" Amber remarked. "Would you tell her it's about time she came back to work? She keeps saying she quit, but with the amount of work that's going to be coming in, we're going to need her help."

"Amber, she's serious about quitting," Capri insisted. "She wants to give this new career of hers a try."

"And how does she think she's going to support herself?" Sighing, Amber threw up her hands in frustration. "This is exactly what happened when she decided she wanted to go into acting. I suppose she'll have to learn the hard way again that dreams don't pay the bills."

"Come on, have some faith in Red," Emerald encouraged Amber. "She's not a teenager anymore. She knows what she's doing and she's good at it, too. I've never seen her work this hard before. She's been stuck in that closet of hers day and night. She's been doing so much recording, she nearly lost her voice."

Devin's mind spun as he digested the women's words. Acting. Closet. Recording. He suddenly remembered the comment Scarlett had made about the book he'd been reading, how it was good in audio form. Audiobook narration—was that what she'd been busy doing this past week when she said she couldn't meet up? "By any chance, does Scarlett narrate books?"

Amber gasped. "You didn't know about this new passion of hers either? At least we're not the only ones she kept out of the loop. Emerald just found out the other day when she overheard Scarlett practicing."

"I thought she was on the phone with you," Emerald explained to Devin, "but then I realized it wasn't likely since she was the only one doing all the talking. I was sure you'd want to get a word in, too. That's when I interrupted her and found out about this hidden talent of hers. I'm surprised she didn't tell you."

"That makes two of us." Devin shook his head in wonder. Why had Scarlett kept something this important from him? Had he been so preoccupied with work that he hadn't taken the time to listen to her? Whatever the reason was, he was determined to let Scarlett know how much he supported her and that she wouldn't have to face anything on her own anymore.

CHAPTER 20
Scarlett

Scarlett felt like the worst girlfriend. Not only had she turned down Devin's marriage proposal, she had also neglected him the past week in favor of doing work. And she'd had the gall to call *him* a workaholic.

Now who was the one eating humble pie again?

Her stomach twisted into knots as she stood outside his house. He had called her last night and asked her over for dinner today. When she'd declined his offer, he had insisted that she at least come for hot chocolate. Scarlett had finally agreed, knowing that she couldn't avoid him forever. But, oh how she wished she could.

Wringing her hands together, she bounced nervously on the balls of her feet. She didn't know how to face Devin after the way she'd disappointed and hurt him. Would he ever forgive her for rejecting him? Was their relationship doomed to fail? How could they salvage it after they'd started off on such a bad note?

Lord, I was supposed to help Devin feel secure in my love, but all I've done is shake his trust. What do I do now?

Scarlett raised her eyes to gaze at the dark sky above. A surprising number of stars were visible, with several lined up together to form a constellation. She was reminded of the verses she'd read that morning from the Book of Psalms about the Lord counting all the stars in the sky and knowing each one by name. Surely God who had such infinite wisdom could help her out of this mess. She just wished she knew what the solution looked like.

The door suddenly swung open, startling Scarlett. Devin's tall frame, in a tan sweater and dark jeans, filled the doorway. His blue eyes swept over her with worry. "What are you doing, Scarlett? You've been standing there for five minutes. Why didn't you ring the doorbell?"

She cringed, realizing he had likely seen every one of her tortured expressions via the video doorbell's camera. Stuffing her hands into the front pocket of her hoodie, she greeted him with a pained smile. "I was going to. I just wasn't ready to face you yet."

His brows furrowed as he pulled her inside and shut the door. "I know I'm not the friendliest person on the planet, but I didn't think I was that unapproachable. What are you talking about?"

"I hurt you, Devin. And I ruined the best thing to have ever happened to me. I don't know how to come back from that. I don't want things to be weird between us, but how can they not when I told you no?"

"I distinctly remember you saying 'not yet.' That's very different from saying no."

"It was still not a yes," she replied adamantly.

His smirk gave way to a dry laugh. "If you're trying to rub it in that you turned down my marriage proposal, you're succeeding."

"That's not what I meant—"

He cut her off with a shake of his head. "You don't have to explain; I understand. I moved too fast. Blame it on my eagerness and impatience. I'm not one to sit around and wait for things to happen; I make them happen. But I realize now that I can't make you trust me. That will have to come with time. Like I told you before, I can wait."

Scarlett's eyes widened to hear his words of assurance. "You really are amazing, Devin. How can you not be taking this personally? If I were you, I'd be devastated."

"Again, you're doing a really good job at making me feel better about the situation." Smirking, he placed his hands on her shoulders and held her gaze. In a kind, patient voice, he continued, "I don't break that easily, Scarlett. I'm also learning to have faith—in God, in you, and in us. You turning me down just shows me how much harder I need to work to show you that I take our relationship very seriously. I'm in this for the long haul. I love you, and I'm committed to you. You've made my every dream come true. I want to help make your dreams come true, too."

She had no idea what she'd done to deserve Devin's support, but she wouldn't take it for granted. His love was such a tangible reminder of God's grace to her. Rewarding him with a teary smile, she wrapped her arms around his waist and hugged him tight. "You know, you're totally winning at this boyfriend game. It must be all the amazing dating advice I gave you."

"Are you trying to take credit for my natural talent?"

With her ear to his chest, she felt the rumble of his laughter as much as she heard it. It was a sound she'd never tire of listening to. "How about I take credit for drawing it out of you? I happen to bring out the best in people," she added as she drew back to face him.

"I'll give you points for that." His eyes sparkled with humor as he grabbed her by the hand. "Come on, there's something I want to show you."

They climbed the carpeted staircase, passing a large chandelier with raindrop-shaped lights that hung from the high ceiling. Once they reached the second story, Devin led her to the first room on the right. Light from the hallway illuminated the dark room, but Scarlett didn't understand what was inside until he flipped on the light.

She covered her mouth in shock. The scene before her looked like a photo from one of her Pinterest boards. Black soundproof foam panels covered most of the red-painted walls of the rectangular space. Sitting against one wall was a large table with all the equipment needed for book narration: a computer, headphones, and a microphone outfitted with both a pop filter and a windscreen. The setup was everything she hoped to have one day for her own home.

She turned to Devin. "What is all this? Why do you have a recording studio in your house?"

"Because I apparently have a girlfriend who narrates books for a living now." His blue eyes narrowed. "When were you going to tell me this important detail? Or were you planning on keeping your identity as S. Haze a secret forever?"

Her brows rose. "How did you know that's me? No one knows my pseudonym name, not even my sisters. I can't believe you figured it out."

"I did have some clues to go on, but I would have appreciated hearing it from you first. Why did you keep this from me? Do you not trust me?"

The hurt in his voice made her chest twinge. "No, it's not that at all. I just wanted to have my act together before I told anyone. This is such a big leap of faith for me, and I have no idea how it's going to pan out. I didn't want to get an 'I told you so' lecture before I even started."

"Hey, I'm not your sisters. I'm here to support you, Scarlett. I listened to your narration last night and was impressed with your work. You have listeners clamoring for more from you. I know you can do this full time. That's why I got this room together. No woman of mine should be stuck doing her recordings in a closet."

She couldn't help but laugh at his incredulous tone. "There's nothing wrong with the closet! I'll have you know that some of the biggest podcasters record in their closets. Soft surfaces like clothing are great at absorbing sound, which is good for the acoustics."

"I doubt it's as good as what you have here. More importantly, this room is big enough to hold two people, so I can come listen to you whenever I want."

"Oh, I see how it is." She playfully poked a finger at his chest. "You want early access to the books I narrate. Is that what this is about?"

"Perhaps, but the main reason is so I'll have you close by." Taking a step closer, he gathered her into his arms and rested his chin on her head. "Now that I've found you, I never want to let you go. I can't imagine my life without you in it."

Her heart swelled. Devin was everything she could have asked for in a man, and more. "You're really racking up the brownie points tonight, Mr. CEO. Thank you so much for this studio and for your sweet encouragement. You're already making my dreams come true, Devin. My love tank is so full, I don't know if there's room for more," she joked as she pulled back to smile at him. "You might need to hold off on those words of affirmation for a while."

"I hope there's at least room for this."

Cradling the nape of her neck, he brought his mouth to meet hers. The kiss started off slow and sweet with a gentle pressure. Scarlett held onto the hem of his sweater, allowing herself to relax in his embrace. His intoxicating, musky scent made her stomach dip and her cheeks flush like a teenager being kissed for the first time. The warmth and strength of his hand splayed on her back provided a sense of security and belonging, two things she had always longed for. She kissed him back with all the confidence and gratitude in her heart, hoping that she could also show Devin how much she cared for him. Just as she was about to deepen their kiss, a phone rang, breaking them apart.

"I need to get this." Devin's expression turned somber as he pulled his phone out of his pocket. "Why don't you get started on the hot chocolate? I'll catch up with you in a few minutes."

He was out of the room before she could reply.

Scarlett didn't think much of Devin's hasty exit until ten, then fifteen minutes had passed, and he still hadn't shown up in the kitchen. She assumed he had a work emergency that needed his attention. As a CEO, he surely had matters to attend to even on the weekends. Whatever the reason for his delay, she decided to bring his cocoa to him. If she waited any longer, their drinks would get cold.

She took the two mugs and walked to Devin's office. Her heart went out to him as she thought about how much responsibility he carried on his shoulders. Even if he didn't want to be a workaholic, his job practically required him to be one. Fortunately, she'd be hanging around here a lot more now that she had a studio she could use. She'd make sure Devin took breaks often.

As she neared the partly open door, the rich timbre of his voice traveled into the hallway. There was an urgency in his tone, bordering on impatience. Gone was the calm, sentimental man from earlier. This was the Devin she remembered meeting a couple of weeks ago, the assertive, no-holds-barred CEO who couldn't be bothered to compromise or change. She couldn't quite grasp how these two, so very different, sides could exist in the same person. The thought left her feeling unsettled yet intrigued. Who was Devin Kendall really?

His voice suddenly grew more upset. She paused, debating whether to enter the room. That's when she heard him say something that made her freeze.

"No, I haven't found a wife yet. I'm working on it, but I need more time."

What in the world was Devin talking about?

CHAPTER 21
Devin

Devin held his head in his hands as he considered the two options his grandfather's lawyer had just presented to him over the phone. Contest the will by calling his grandfather's mental capacity into question or get married. Both choices were impossible and wrong, given the circumstances. He couldn't lie and tarnish his grandfather's reputation, nor could he pressure Scarlett into marrying him. The only other solution was a leveraged buyout. He would need to convince his cousin Nick to sell his control of the company to him, then secure a loan to afford the purchase. He would be heavily in debt, but if that was the only way to save Kendall & Sons, so be it.

His chest heaved with each breath he released. The hardest part of this situation was knowing that he was in it alone. He couldn't ask his siblings for advice. They would likely tell him to let the company go, or worse, to work for Nick and watch everything he'd help build crash and burn to the ground. He also couldn't involve the one person he longed to confide in the most —Scarlett. Telling her the terms of the will would no doubt push her into a corner. It was too much, too soon. He'd need to figure this out himself. But first, he needed to pray.

I'm at the end of my rope, God. I could really use Your help.

Turning to the Lord in times of need wasn't his usual first inclination, but he had no other choice. But perhaps this was the best dilemma to be in—one in which he was forced to rely on God, which was how he ought to be living regardless of the circumstance. This was his one consolation, aside from the fact that he had Scarlett by his side.

He glanced at his watch, realizing he'd left her waiting. Standing to his feet, he was about to go find her when he heard a soft knock on the door.

"Can I come in?" Scarlett asked as she stepped inside. "I brought our drinks."

"Of course." He joined her on the couch and took the mug she offered him. The room seemed warmer with her in it, and it wasn't because she'd brought him hot chocolate. Scarlett's mere presence was enough to chase away his worries. He stretched one arm along the back of the couch and tried to relax. "I'm sorry I made you wait. The call took a lot longer than I anticipated."

"Was it about work? Did something urgent come up?"

He nodded as he took a sip of the sweet drink. "Yes, but nothing that can't be resolved. Don't worry about it. I'll deal with it later."

"Are you sure? You can talk to me about it. I'm pretty good at listening."

"Thank you, but I'm sure. I wouldn't want to bore you with the details."

"I don't mind, really. I feel like there's a lot I don't know about you yet that I should know."

"I'm sure there is, given how new our relationship is. The familiarity will come with time. We have the rest of our lives to get to know each other better."

She furrowed her brows, not seeming satisfied with his answer. "But it's better to find out some things earlier than later. I'd like to ask you some questions now, if you don't mind."

Devin cocked his head, curious as to the change in Scarlett's tone and appearance. Her whole demeanor was more serious than usual. Despite her casual clothing, she kept her back stiff and straight. He had no idea what was going on in her head. "Are you upset that I made you wait?"

"No, that's not what's bothering me."

"So, something is bothering you. What is it?"

"I just need to clear some things up."

"Go for it. Ask me whatever you want."

"What made you decide to sign up with a matchmaking service? Were you hoping to get married soon?"

He blinked, surprised by her line of questioning. "Why do you ask?"

"I just wonder why someone as busy as you would be interested in dating. You don't go out for fun on your own, so why would you want to go out with someone else for fun? It doesn't make sense why you'd put yourself through this whole experience unless there was a good reason to do so. So, why did you sign up?"

Her green eyes sparkled with fervor, an obvious sign that she wasn't letting this go. But why did it matter so much to her? And why now? He weighed his words, wondering what Scarlett wanted to hear. "You're right, I didn't sign up because I wanted to date. The fact of the matter is, I don't have time to go out for pleasure. I had hoped the matchmaking process would be straightforward and efficient and require the least amount of effort on my part."

"But why? You're still not answering my question, Mr. Kendall."

"Mr. Kendall?" He frowned. "Why do I feel like I'm being interrogated here?"

"Because I feel like you're keeping something from me. You keep dodging my questions. Why do you need to get married?"

He realized what was going on. "You heard me talking on the phone, didn't you?"

"Yes, but it wasn't on purpose, I promise. The door was open, and I happened to overhear you."

"It's fine, but what exactly did you overhear?"

"You said you hadn't found a wife yet, but you were working on it." She chewed her lower lip before asking, "What's going on, Devin? What did you mean when you said you were working on it? Am I some kind of pet project for you? Do you have a bet you're trying to win?"

"That's not what's happening. I can explain."

"Go on, I'm listening."

Sighing, he set his mug on the side table, then turned around to face her. This was not the way he'd imagined this evening going. All he'd wanted was to have a peaceful night with Scarlett where they could enjoy each other's company after a long week apart. He'd wanted to show her how much he believed in her skills and talent as a narrator. The last thing he desired was to open up Pandora's box, but here they were. He had no choice but to tell her the truth.

"I did sign up for your service so I could find a wife. There's a stipulation in my grandfather's will that says his company can only be inherited by an heir who is married. I believe his intentions were good when he wrote it. He had made it clear that he wanted me to take over the business, but he also worried that I worked too much. I assume that's why he added in that clause. The problem now is that my cousin who has absolutely no interest in the company is threatening to take it over. Since he's married and I'm not, it will automatically go to him. But you should know that none of this has anything to do with you and me. I want to be with you regardless of this situation, Scarlett. That's the truth."

Her complexion paled as she stared up at him. "You'll lose your CEO position if you don't have a wife? When do you need to get married by?"

"By the first of January."

"In two months?!"

"Yes."

Hurt registered in her eyes. "So that's why you proposed."

"No! That was not the reason why. I asked you to marry me because I want to spend the rest of my life with you, not because of some clause. You have to believe me."

"I want to, but ..." Several different emotions flashed across her face like the bolts of a lightning storm. Her voice wavered as she continued, "I-I don't know what to believe. Put yourself in my shoes. Wouldn't you be wary of everything that's happened? You proposed a week after we got together, Devin. I don't want to question your intentions—"

"Then don't question them. Trust me, Scarlett."

In an instant, her shoulders slouched, making her look small and unsure. Her confidence and boldness vanished, and she stopped making eye contact. "I can't help but wonder if this was your plan all along. Maybe you realized the matches I found for you were too smart to fall for you in such a short amount of time, so you decided to target me instead. You knew I'd been manipulated by my ex before, and you thought you could get to me, too. It all makes sense when you think about it," she muttered more to herself than to him. "I can't believe I got fooled again so easily."

"Scarlett, stop." He took her mug and set it aside, then grabbed onto her hands. "You're spiraling, sweetheart. Take a minute to think this through. If I was only invested in finding a wife, I wouldn't have told you I'd wait for you. I wouldn't have set up a recording studio for you in my home. I wouldn't have called my grandfather's lawyer to ask what other options I have. That's why I was on the phone for so long. I wanted to know what else I could do because the last thing I want is to pressure you to do something you don't want to do. I would never let you sacrifice your interests and happiness for me. That's what my mother did for my father, and it—it broke her." His voice faltered as his throat grew raw. "I won't let that happen to you, Scarlett. You have my word."

Devin didn't know if what he said was enough. He could only pray that it was, that Scarlett would trust his words and give him a chance to prove them. Bringing her hands to his lips, he placed a soft kiss on each of her palms. He tried to keep his composure, but the ache in his chest made it hard to breathe. He'd never had so much on the line. He could find a way to salvage his family's company, but whether Scarlett would have him was completely out of his control.

Whatever happened now was in God's hands. He would need to accept that.

He dropped his gaze to his lap where their hands lay. Scarlet's slender fingers were laced with his, a symbolic display of how her life had intersected with his. They fit together so effortlessly, he wanted to believe they were meant for each other. But as the silence between them dragged on, Devin could sense she was struggling. He decided to make it easier for her.

Painfully and reluctantly, he pulled his hands away. He raised his head and found her regarding him with tears in her eyes. "I understand why you'd want to break up with me. You don't have to explain—"

"Devin, I'm not breaking up with you. But I need time to process everything that's happened. Please give me a few days. I'll call you when I'm ready to talk."

Scarlett then left the room, taking all the warmth and hope with her, and leaving Devin to wonder when he'd see her again.

CHAPTER 22
Scarlett

Had she made the same mistake again? Did she fall for a guy who was just using her to advance his career? Scarlett couldn't shake the weariness weighing on her heart as she questioned everything she knew about Devin. Or everything she thought she knew about him. What and who was she supposed to believe?

Five days had passed since she'd told Devin she needed time. She'd kept herself busy with narrating, volunteering, and whatever else she could do that would prevent her mind from spiraling. Devin had been right; once she allowed herself to doubt, that's all she could focus on.

But how could she stop doubting?

Usually in times like this when she was confused or unsure, she'd go to her sisters for advice. Amber, as direct as she was, always had something logical to say. Capri had a soft heart and tried to think the best of people. Emerald was generous with her hugs and a listening ear. Her sisters were her sounding boards and voices of reason. But she didn't want to bring another mess to them that they needed to fix. She'd caused enough trouble already.

Instead, she'd brought them lunch from their favorite salad

and sandwich shop, along with homemade cookies and a heartfelt apology. Now all she needed to do was work up enough courage to open the door to Party of Two.

God, please help me patch things up with them.

After her prayer, Scarlett stepped inside, buoyed by a cool gust of wind that blew the door wide open. It ruffled the hem of her long gray cardigan that she wore over a pair of jeans. Her hands full, she looked up in relief to see Emerald rush over to help her close the door.

"Red! You got us lunch? You're the best!"

Not more than five seconds later, both Amber and Capri emerged from their individual offices.

"Do I smell snickerdoodles?" Capri exclaimed. "This all looks so good. Thanks, Red!"

"Yes, thank you, sis." Amber greeted her with a genuine smile. "This saves us a lot of time. We still have so much to do with our hair and makeup and tidying this place up."

"You guys aren't mad at me?" Scarlett blinked in surprise at their friendly greeting. "Wait, what do you mean, 'hair and makeup'? What's going on?"

"For our interview. The news crew will be here in an hour," Capri said in between bites of her sandwich. "Didn't Devin tell you?"

Scarlett shrugged, then took a seat beside Emerald on the loveseat by the wall. "He didn't mention it. Is this related to the news article? Wouldn't an interview be giving more negative press for Party of Two?"

Amber shook her head. "No, this is a good thing. KRON's coming to do a special segment on matchmaking for the holidays. I thought you were the one who gave him the idea. When he stopped by last week, he said he came on behalf of the two of you. You really had no idea about this?"

"He said he had something in the works to help the business out, but I didn't know what it was."

"You found a good one, Red." Capri grinned with approval. "It's clear that he loves you. He came in here like a man on a mission and blew us all away with a speech about how you changed his life for the better."

"He did? What did he say exactly?"

"Stuff like how you drove him crazy, but he couldn't get you off his mind. My favorite part was about how you not only make him want to be a better man, but you give him the confidence to be one." Capri clutched her chest with one hand, pretending to swoon. "Isn't that so romantic?"

Scarlett couldn't believe her ears. Devin had truly gone above and beyond, not only with helping the business but also getting on her sisters' good side. And he had done both without her knowledge, which meant he wasn't looking for brownie points. On the other hand, maybe he was and hoped that the news would travel back to her—as it just had—so he could convince her to marry him. Scarlett's thoughts bounced back and forth like a tennis ball, wavering between wanting to see Devin as a hero or as a villain. Why couldn't she be more sure? What else would it take for her to trust him?

"I'm surprised he said those things," she simply replied.

"He did, and he even won *me* over, which is not an easy feat as you know." Amber smirked. "It's obvious why he fell for you, Red, but I understand now why you fell for him, too. As for your other question, no, we're not mad at you. At least not anymore."

This was the reconciliation she'd come here for. Scarlett went around and gave each of them a hug. "I'm sorry again for making such a mess of things. I didn't mean to cause trouble or more work for you guys. I hope you'll forgive me."

"It's all good."

"Don't worry about it."

Capri and Emerald chimed in, their tones pleasant. Scarlett looked over at Amber, hoping she'd be as gracious.

"All is forgiven," Amber declared, "including our bet."

The knot in Scarlett's stomach loosened. "Thank you!"

"Although, I think you technically won," Capri stated. "You *were* the first one to find your client a match. We never specified who the match could or couldn't be."

"Which means the three of us would need to shave our eyebrows," Emerald admitted with a grimace. "So, I agree that all is forgiven."

Amber nodded. "You're more than welcome to come back to work, Red. Business is bound to pick up after this news segment airs, and we could really use your expertise. How sure are you about this career change that you're making?"

"It's the only thing I'm sure about right now. I love matchmaking, and I'll probably come back to it someday, but for now, I'm really enjoying narration. I get to work in my pjs all day and bake whenever I want to. And Devin set up a recording studio for me in his house, too, that I can't wait to use," she added with forced enthusiasm.

"Why do you sound so unhappy then?" Emerald asked, picking up on the strain in her voice. "What are you not telling us?"

Scarlett's chest tightened. Hearing that her sisters approved of Devin meant so much to her, but what would they think if they knew the whole story? Wringing her hands together, she sighed. "I didn't say anything because I wanted to figure this out on my own, but I could use some advice. You guys are always good at steering me in the right direction."

"That's what we're here for," Amber insisted, "so you don't have to make the same mistakes we did. So, spill. Is this about you and Devin?"

"Yes." She filled her sisters in on everything that had happened in the past couple of weeks, including the clause in Devin's grandfather's will and Devin's marriage proposal. The more she talked, the quieter her sisters became. By the end of her sharing, they had all stopped eating in favor of listening. She raised her palms up and shrugged. "Do you guys see my dilemma now? I just want to know if Devin wants to be with me for me and not because he needs a wife to save his job. How do I know for sure?"

Capri spoke up first. "What does your heart tell you? How do you feel when you're with him?"

"Amazing. I feel loved and respected and supported." Scarlett's words sprung forth without effort. "Devin makes me happy, and I think I make him happy, too. It just feels right when we're together."

"That sounds great and all," Amber remarked with her no-nonsense attitude, "but feelings are the last thing you should be relying on. Forget feelings. Let's consider the facts. How do you know Devin is committed? What has he done to show you that he is?"

"He's done so much. He stood up for me in front of Conrad. He put the studio together for me to use anytime I want to. He left work early to come see me when I was in the middle of one of my baking meltdowns. And he literally wants to spend the rest of his life with me. I don't know how much more he could do to show me his commitment."

"Don't forget the part where he may be single-handedly saving our business," Emerald added.

"The interview!" Amber and Capri both exclaimed and jumped to their feet, quickly stuffing the last bites of their food into their mouths.

"Sorry, Red, we need to get ready." Capri gave her a hug and an apologetic smile. "Don't think too much about this. Just go with your heart."

"But do try to use your head more." Amber arched one brow with the unspoken authority of an older sister. "Take your time. You'll figure it out."

"That's it?" Scarlett protested, waving her hands in the air. Her sisters were halfway down the hall when she tried one final attempt. "You guys don't have any more advice for me?"

Emerald walked over and gave her a comforting pat on the shoulder. "You've got this, Red. If you can hold your ground with a guy like Devin, you don't need us to tell you what to do. I promise to pray for you, but right now I really need to fix my lipstick. Thanks again for lunch!"

In a matter of seconds, Scarlett found herself alone in the waiting area. She sighed loudly as she considered her options. Part of her felt like she was in the middle of one of those choose your own adventure books she used to read as a child. Go to page 23 if you trust Devin or go to page 76 if you don't. If only she had the option of peeking at both pages to see which path was safer. Without the ability to look ahead, how could she be sure she was making a wise choice?

Lord, please give me wisdom to make the choice that's safe and right and the best for me—

Her prayer abruptly stopped. The best—that's what she'd asked God for. But what did *the best* even mean? Would she be spared from trouble or hurt? Not a chance. Every marriage had its share of disagreements and challenges—even the wonderful one her grandparents had had.

Scarlett's heart thumped in her chest. She realized she'd gotten it all wrong. It wasn't Devin she didn't trust, it was herself.

The reason why she kept second-guessing him was because of her past experiences. She still judged herself harshly for everything that had happened with Conrad. For her foolishness in ignoring all the red flags she saw and her naivety in thinking that she could change him—she hadn't let herself off the hook for any of it. As a result, she didn't trust her own judgment. That mistrust had colored her view of Devin and made her jump to conclusions about his motives. But when she took everything into consideration—from her sisters' input to the peace she felt when she was with him—there were no red flags to speak of. Aside from her grandfather and dad, Devin was the best man she'd ever met.

The best—that's exactly what she had prayed for. And God,

being all knowing and all loving, had answered her prayer before she'd even asked.

Thank You, Lord!

"Are you still here, Red?" Emerald emerged from the hall wearing a fresh coat of lipstick and mascara. When she spotted Scarlett, a bright smile appeared on her face. "Oh good, you haven't left yet."

"You look great, Em. Do you need help with something?"

"I wanted to tell you that I had an a-ha moment when I was praying just now. I thought there was something different about you, and I realized what it was. It's your eyes."

"My eyes? I don't have makeup on today."

Emerald laughed. "That's not what I meant. It was when you were talking about Devin—the look in your eyes was different. I saw confidence in them. I don't remember you being like that with Conrad. With him, it always seemed like you were trying to prove yourself, prove that you were good enough to be with him. You looked tired and sad most of the time. It's not the same with Devin though. I get the feeling he makes you feel secure. That's the kind of guy I want to see you with."

"He does make me feel secure." There was no hesitation in Scarlett's answer. Knowing that Emerald could see the difference between these two relationships helped cement her plan. "Thanks for telling me this. I've figured out what I'm going to do."

"Let me guess. You're going to go find Devin and tell him how much you love him and want to have his babies? *After* you marry him, of course," she added with a wink.

"You read my mind!"

That's when Scarlett decided that Devin wouldn't be the only one who could propose.

CHAPTER 23

Devin

Go big or go home.

This was Devin's mentality when it came to saving Kendall & Sons from his cousin. Unfortunately, all the effort he had put in this week so far had been for naught. Nick refused to sell the company—despite the exorbitant amount Devin had offered him—and the board was unwilling to go against his grandfather's will and keep Devin on as CEO. He had just about run out of options at this point. The only thing he had left was a mustard seed of faith that God might turn things around, but even that was on the verge of being crushed by doubt.

What he needed was a miracle, and he needed it now.

He stared up at the undercarriage of the older model Porsche he had been adjusting the spark plugs on. The smell of grease and oil filled his nostrils as he took a deep breath. Working on this car usually gave him a sense of calm, but he had too much adrenaline running through his veins to settle down.

The stress and worries of the situation were wearing on him. He'd had to leave the office early when his head had started to pound with the beginnings of a migraine. Even a workout at the gym hadn't helped.

Lord, I'm running out of time. Would You help me figure this out, and soon? And would you take care of Scarlett for me?

This had been Devin's prayer every day, several times a day. While talking to God had become easier the more often he did it, waiting on Him was a different matter. This was the ultimate test in trust. Devin could only hope that God would answer his prayers before his patience ran out.

The door connecting the house to the garage suddenly opened and shut with a clicking sound. He recognized the rhythm and pacing of the approaching footsteps like they were his own.

"Hey Dev, there you are. When do I get to meet this girlfriend of yours? Any chance she's coming by today?"

At the sound of his brother's voice, Devin slid the under-car creeper he was lying on out from under the car. His eyes adjusted to the late afternoon sun streaming in through the open garage door before focusing on Jace's enthusiastic grin. He'd had his hair cut short and started growing out his beard, two things he did every time he returned to what he called "civilian life" to hide his identity. The two of them looked more alike today than they had in months.

Jace had only returned from tour yesterday, but Bekah had already updated him on everything he'd missed while he was gone. He seemed especially interested in Devin's relationship and hadn't stopped asking about Scarlett. Devin wished he had an answer to give him. It had been five long and lonely days without a single word from her. He wasn't sure how much longer he could refrain from reaching out. He understood her need for time and space, but he only grew more concerned the longer she stayed away. If he weren't getting daily updates from Bekah, he would have knocked down Scarlett's door already. "I don't expect to see her today."

"Huh. If Bekah didn't know her personally, I'd wonder if you made her up." Jace leaned back against the large tool cabinet sitting against one wall, his posture slouched and relaxed. He narrowed his blue eyes and pinned his gaze on Devin. "You only work on this old clunker when you're upset. Are you having trouble in paradise already?"

Devin sighed. Having his twin around was akin to hearing his thoughts spoken out loud. Jace could read him like a book without having to turn the pages. At least this made it easier to cut out the small talk. He wiped his hands on his grease-stained jeans, debating how much of the situation to share with Jace now that he didn't have his tour to focus on. Was that a wise thing to do though? Why burden his brother with something he couldn't do anything about?

"If you're worried about burdening me with your problems," Jace remarked, as if he'd read Devin's mind, "don't be. I'm a big boy, Dev. You don't have to protect me anymore. I can handle it. You'll feel a lot better once you get whatever's bothering you off your chest."

"When did you start talking like a shrink?"

"Since I started seeing one." The smirk that appeared on Jace's face was identical to his own. "Pretend I'm yours. What's going on with you?"

Something about his brother seemed different, more stable and mature. Perhaps the therapist he'd been seeing recently was helping. Devin inhaled, feeling the weight on his shoulders ease a bit. It felt strange to have the tables turned, but having Jace offer to listen made it a bit easier to open up. "It's complicated, to say the least."

"Isn't it always when it involves a woman?"

"Yeah, well, this involves the company, too." He went on to reveal the clause in their grandfather's will, their cousin's threat, his backfired marriage proposal, and Scarlett's response to it all. "Now the ball's in her court," he concluded with a weariness in his voice. "There's nothing I can do but wait."

"I can't believe you've been keeping all that to yourself, Dev.

No wonder you're stressed out. Why didn't you tell me about the will?"

"Why would I? You've never been interested in taking over the business. You have your own career to worry about."

"True, but there's gotta be some other way I can help you out." He rubbed his jaw as he thought. "What if I became the CEO—in name only of course—while you did the actual job? It'd be like hiring a ghostwriter—I would be the face and you would be the brains. You could even pretend to be me at the office; no one would ever notice. We used to get away with trading places all the time."

Devin eyed him warily. "It worked when we were kids. We haven't traded places in years."

"Who says it can't work now? It would just be a temporary solution anyway. Once Scarlett's ready to marry you, I'd step down and you'd take over again. That's a brilliant plan, if I do say so myself."

He couldn't help but smile at Jace's boyish enthusiasm. "That sounds great and all, but do you happen to have a wife hidden somewhere that I don't know about?"

"Not right this moment, but I could easily find a woman who'd agree to a contract marriage with me. I already get dozens of proposals every day. I'd just have to accept one of them."

"You're talking about a marriage on paper?" Devin shook his head in dismay at his brother's cavalier attitude. Jace had spouted off the suggestion as if he were talking about leasing a car. Perhaps he hadn't changed as much as he'd thought. "I appreciate the offer, but I would never ask you to make that kind of sacrifice. Marriage is sacred, Jace. You can't turn it into a contract and put an expiration date on it, no matter how desperate the circumstances are. No, I won't let you do that. A contract marriage is off the table."

"All right, all right, no contract marriage. I was half joking, Dev," Jace exclaimed, his tone one of chagrin. "You're still as intense as ever, but your priorities have changed. Weren't you the one who always said, if something is important to you, you have to make the necessary sacrifices? The old you would have found a way around this problem by now with no questions asked. You would do everything in your power to make sure Nick doesn't win. The two of you have been competing since you were kids. I can't believe you're backing down now. Who are you, and what have you done with my brother?"

Devin had been pondering that very question himself. He ran his thumb along the spark plug feeler gauge in his hand, feeling the weight of its 32 metal blades on his palm. His grandfather had passed this tool, along with a passion for cars and the family business, on to him when he was still a boy. And now he was contemplating giving up the latter, for what—love? Would he regret the decision one day? What if Nick ran the company to the ground and destroyed everything his grandfather had built? How would he deal with the guilt then? Or on the off chance that Nick succeeded as CEO, would he be able to sit by and watch him gloat and not let bitterness and resentment tear him apart?

Shaking his head, he looked up to meet Jace's gaze. "Honestly, I don't know what's happened to me. This decision should be an easy one to make, but I can't bring myself to put aside my emotions and act on logic alone. I won't give up on what I have with Scarlett."

Jace surprised him by grinning. "You know what? That has got to be the most sincere thing you've ever said in your life. You're making a decision based on what you want instead of what you think you *should* do. I'm proud of you, bro."

He scoffed, more out of amusement than anything. His brother was giving *him* a pep talk? Obviously, he wasn't the only one doing some changing. "Thanks. I'm not going down without a fight though. Kendall & Sons was important to Grandfather, and it's also important to me. I won't stand by and watch Nick bring it down."

Rubbing the scruff along his jawline, Jace mused. "That's the part that doesn't make sense to me. Why would Grandad put the whole company on the line just to make sure you get married? Did he think you're that stubborn—" He cut himself off with a laugh. "Never mind, I answered my own question."

"He was just as stubborn," Devin noted. "Once he got an idea in his head, no one could change his mind."

"Except Grammy." Jace's brows rose in understanding. "I get it now. Grandad wanted you to have a woman by your side who could talk some sense into you, like Grammy did for him. It makes total sense why he put that clause in his will."

"Sure, but it would have worked out better if he hadn't included a deadline for the marriage."

"You can't put the blame on Grandad for that. You've had almost a whole year to get married. You should've started your search for a wife months ago."

Devin shot him a disgruntled look. "Thanks for stating the obvious. I know that part is my fault. That's why I'm paying the consequences for it now."

"Wow." Jace's jaw dropped. "I can count on one hand the number of times you've admitted you were wrong. You really have changed, Dev. I bet we have Scarlett to thank for that."

The mention of Scarlett again brought her beautiful green eyes to mind. Devin clenched his hands, wishing he could reach out to her. He needed to know how she was doing. How much more time did she need? What more could he do to convince her that his intentions were true?

That was when it came to him. He needed to demonstrate his commitment to Scarlett in a way that would leave no room for doubt.

Devin jumped to his feet, then tossed the tool in his hand to his brother. "I need to make a call."

"To Scarlett?"

"No, to the Board Chair. Pray for me, will you? I'll explain later."

"When did you start praying again?"

Jace's voice faded as Devin stepped inside the house. He'd tell his brother about his renewed faith in God later, but now he had some convincing to do.

CHAPTER 24
Scarlett

Had Devin been this nervous at the ice-skating rink?

Scarlett clutched her steering wheel with damp hands and turned the AC on full blast. Beads of sweat lined her forehead as she maneuvered her sedan through the neighborhood street leading to Devin's home. She forced her lungs to work as her heart pounded.

The more she thought about her plan, the crazier it sounded. What was she thinking? She hadn't spoken to Devin all week and now she was going over to propose to him? Sure, he had already proposed to her, but she had turned him down. What if he also rejected her? Scarlett had no idea what he currently thought of her or their relationship, and it was this uncertainty that made her want to stop the car and make a U-turn.

Lord, please give me Your wisdom and peace. Help me to have the right words to say to Devin.

She continued driving until a large two-story Spanish-style house with its manicured lawn and brick walkway came into view. Straightening her posture, she held her head up high. She couldn't back out now, not when she was here, and certainly not when Devin's family business was at stake. While their jobs and lines of work were different, she understood the pressures he faced. He wasn't only working for himself, he had people to answer to. His grandfather had expected him to oversee the company. He had thousands of employees who relied on the business's success for their paychecks. This situation was so much bigger than just the two of them.

Still, even if this didn't involve the clause in his grandfather's will, Scarlett was certain now of where she stood. This was an act of commitment and faith on her part, in the Lord's plans, in Devin, and in their future together. She trusted God and believed He had brought her and Devin together. She also trusted Devin. Everything that she knew about him, from what she had observed to what Bekah had told her, rang true. He was a man of integrity and compassion.

I can wait.

Those three words that Devin had spoken to her came to mind, bringing with them a sense of calm. How wonderful it would be for him to truly be waiting for her. She pictured him at his front door greeting her with his arms open wide. She was ready to jump into his embrace and feel his love in a tangible way again.

Her nerves would disappear once she saw Devin, she was sure of it.

She pulled up the paved driveway on the right-hand side of the house to where one of two garage doors was open. Turning off the engine, she checked her reflection in the rearview mirror one last time. She'd made a special effort to look her best for this occasion. The shimmery gold and copper shades of her eye shadow complemented her nude-colored lipstick. Her long hair fell in loose curls around her shoulders, skimming the spaghetti straps of her burgundy dress. Releasing a long breath, she adjusted the sash around her waist and smoothed down the flowy fabric of the skirt. Her outfit was perfect for a romantic date, which she hoped would be the outcome of this evening.

When she stepped out of her car, she spotted an older

vehicle parked inside the garage with its hood up. A pair of large feet clad in sneakers poked out from underneath it. Scarlett smiled at the sight, knowing that Devin was a mere five feet away. Her worries lifted and all she felt was peace and excitement. She quickly walked over, the clicking of her heels announcing her arrival.

"Hi, Devin, it's me," she called out as she reached his side. She knelt down, anticipating his reaction. Would there be a smile on his handsome face or a frown? She would take either one at this point, if only just to see him again.

He rolled out from under the car in one swift motion, then sat up to face her. His expression was one of surprise mixed with curiosity, as if he were seeing her for the first time. "You look amazing. I didn't think you were coming by today."

The knot in Scarlett's stomach loosened at his compliment. His tone was as casual as his jeans and T-shirt. The way his eyes lit up set her even more at ease. She reached over and placed her hand on his. "I'm so sorry I didn't call you sooner. It took me some time to figure things out, but I'm good now—great, actually. I've been praying and I talked to my sisters, and I see the situation clearly now. I know what I want, Devin, and what I want is—wait a minute..."

Scarlett withdrew her hand, cautiously studying the man before her. His haircut and beard were the same as Devin's, but there was a glint in his eyes that she wasn't used to seeing. It carried an element of playfulness and warmth unlike Devin's usual demeanor. The Devin she had fallen in love with was fervent to the core. He didn't do anything half-heartedly. The longer she stared, the more certain she was that this man was not her boyfriend.

She stood up and crossed her arms. Going with her gut, she exclaimed, "You're Jace, aren't you? I can't believe I almost proposed—"

The door to the house swung open at the same time, cutting

off her words. Scarlett looked over and raised her hands in a celebratory dance when she spotted the real Devin.

Her Devin.

"I was right!" She ran over and threw her arms around him. "It's you, it's really you!"

"Sweetheart, you're here," he murmured in her ear before pulling back to look at her. "Of course, it's me. Who else would I ..." His eyes widened with realization. "You thought Jace was me."

"Only for a second, bro." Jace chuckled as he made his way past them. He paused to give Devin a pat on the shoulder and a nod of approval. "She saw right through me, which was no easy feat. Congrats, Dev, it looks like you'll be able to keep your job after all. And welcome to the family, Scarlett! I look forward to getting to know the woman who won over my brother," he added with a wink before stepping into the house.

Devin's brows drew together as his eyes darkened with intensity. "What was that all about? Care to fill me in on what I missed?"

Scarlett's heart did a happy little flip. There was the man she adored. She grabbed Devin's hands, unable to stop smiling. She knew exactly what she wanted to say. "You didn't miss much, but you did miss hearing me apologize for not calling you all week. I'm sorry I made you wait so long, Devin."

"It doesn't matter. All that matters is that you're here now." He brought one of her hands to his lips for a kiss. "Is that it?"

She shook her head. "The other thing you missed was me saying that I've finally figured things out. I have an answer to the question you asked me before."

"Which question is that?"

"You asked me what I want in life."

"And what is it that you want, sweetheart?"

"I want to spend the rest of my days with the man I love. That's you, Devin. I want to do life with you and build a home and a family with you, too. I want to be the one to go to Golfland with you someday and hear you tell our kids the story of how you and I fell in love there. What I'm saying is, I want to be your wife. So—" She took a deep breath and asked, "Devin Kendall, will you marry me?"

He held her gaze, unblinking. "You're proposing to me?"

"I am. Do you have a problem with that? There's no rule that says a woman can't propose to a man."

"I have no problem with you proposing. But the thing is, I already proposed to you, and my proposal still stands. It's only fair that you answer me first."

A hint of a smile played on Devin's lips, making her eyes roll. "Are you serious? This isn't a competition, Mr. CEO."

"I know it isn't. It's a matter of principle." He wrapped an arm around her waist and drew her close. "You're trying to answer a question with a question. I'd like an answer."

Scarlett threw her head back and laughed. Oh, how she'd missed their banter. There was no question about it—she'd met her match. She loved that they could have fun together like this. She also loved that Devin was someone she could respect and support and be respected and supported in return. There was no fear of losing herself when she knew Devin wanted the best for her. Because of this security that he offered, Scarlett could easily and readily back down. "Okay, you win. Yes, I will marry you! We can get married before the end of the year and you can keep your job!"

Devin remained silent, his expression unreadable. Scarlett considered it a small victory that she could make him speechless, but when he still hadn't spoken after several seconds, she grew concerned. "Devin, did you hear me? I said yes."

He cleared his throat and nodded. His voice resonated with emotion as he replied, "I heard you. Thank you, sweetheart. I'm just overwhelmed by your support. I know this takes a tremendous amount of faith on your part to trust me enough to say yes."

"You make it easy to, Devin. I do trust you, and I trust the

Lord, too. I believe He brought us together so we could help each other learn and grow. It's all part of His good and perfect plan for us."

"I couldn't agree more. You won't be surprised then when I tell you that God already worked out a solution for us that didn't require either one of us to propose."

"What do you mean?"

"I just got off the phone with the Board Chairman. I was up front about our situation, how I had found the woman I want to be my wife, but we need more time before getting married, and as a result, I was ready to give my notice. I then asked if he would consider bringing me onto the board so I could have some say over how Kendall & Sons would be run when my cousin took over. That's when he told me my grandfather had added a hidden clause to his will for this very scenario. If I decided to forego my job for the sake of love, I would automatically inherit the company." He shook his head and chuckled. "Grandad really covered all the bases. He thought of everything."

Scarlett's eyes filled with tears. As thankful as she was for Devin's grandfather's foresight, she was more grateful for Devin's sacrificial heart. "I can't believe you were going to give up your job for me. I don't know what to say."

He ran the pad of his thumb across her cheek and wiped away a tear. "You don't have to say anything. I'm the one who should be thanking you. You saved me, Scarlett. You brought hope and faith back into my life. I'm not the same man I used to be, and it's all because of you. Thank you."

She smiled through her tears of joy. "I did my job well, didn't I? I told you I'd find you your perfectly imperfect match."

"I'd have to disagree with that statement." Before Scarlett could open her mouth to protest, Devin went on to explain. "You *are* the perfect match for me. I couldn't ask for anything more. Except for one thing."

"What's that?"

"That I could have been the one to see you first tonight." He tightened his hold on her until they were flush against each other. His voice grew husky with appreciation. "You look incredible, sweetheart. I may like this dress more than your pajamas."

She laughed. "You like my froggy pajamas? I'll have to buy you a matching set. It'll be my engagement gift to you."

"Speaking of engagement gifts—" Devin reached into his pocket and pulled out a ring box. "Let me give you yours. I've been carrying this around with me all week and praying for a chance to give it to you again."

She held out her left hand and watched with anticipation as Devin slipped the solitaire ring onto her finger. With the darkening night sky as their backdrop, the diamond sparkled like a star. It shone like the hope that was blooming in her heart. There was so much to look forward to in their future together, and she couldn't wait to get started.

Smiling up at Devin, she laced her fingers with his. "What do you think of an outdoor wedding? I know the weather's cooling down, but maybe we could rent some heat lamps and pass out hot chocolate."

"Hold on, you're not still thinking of getting married before the new year? There's no need to rush anymore. I'm staying on as CEO."

"I know. But getting married sooner would be so much more convenient. I could use the recording studio whenever I want to without having to drive over."

He quirked a brow. "So, you're marrying me for the studio?"

She pretended to ponder his question. "Not only for the studio. Your kitchen is pretty great, too. I've never had two ovens before. It makes baking so much faster."

"You're marrying me for the studio and the kitchen?" he asked drolly. "Is that all?"

"Of course not. Marrying you means Bekah and I will be

sisters. We'll get to have girls' night in together all the time. It'll be so much fun!"

Devin pursed his lips, clearly unamused by her teasing. "If I didn't know better, I'd think you were marrying me for my money and connections. And all this time, I thought you liked me for my hotness."

Scarlett laughed. The sparkle in his blue eyes lit up his whole face and made her heart happy. She raised herself on her tiptoes and leaned closer until their mouths met. The fresh scent of his aftershave awakened her senses as her lips moved over his, tenderly leaving traces of love with each touch. Devin returned her kisses with an equal amount of passion, softly at first, then with more urgency until he had her back pressed against the car. Her knees weakened as heat rushed through her body, leaving tingles in its wake.

When they finally pulled apart, breathless and flushed, she remarked playfully, "I am definitely marrying you for your hotness."

He then kissed her again in the same way that she knew he did everything—with his whole heart.

Epilogue
DEVIN

Like Scarlett had envisioned, they held an intimate outdoor wedding the day after Christmas. The ceremony took place at Cowell's Beach in Santa Cruz, complete with heat lamps and a hot cocoa and coffee bar. With their families and close friends as witnesses, they made their vows to one another as the sun dipped below the horizon. Shortly afterwards, they took the celebration indoors to the neighboring Dream Inn where they ate dinner with a stunning panoramic view of the ocean.

He and Scarlett shared the long rectangular head table with her parents and their siblings. The mood was lighthearted and jovial and the conversation nonstop. Scarlett's young cousins were a source of amusement with their antics and questions. Devin found himself loosening up and laughing, two things he had been learning to do more of since Scarlett came into his life.

In the time that they had been together, he rarely brought his work home with him. His evenings were for "living," as Scarlett called it. Oftentimes they listened to audiobooks, played miniature golf (one of their favorite pastimes), or baked cookies and pies, an activity that Scarlett now did for enjoyment. Devin had also gotten her familiar with the underhood of a car, teaching her how to change its oil and adjust its spark plugs. A couple of weekends had been spent at the zoo and the ice-skating rink as well as trying new things such as cooking classes. They had been sharing their worlds with each other for the past couple of months, and now that they were married, they could officially do so for the rest of their lives.

This wedding reception was only the beginning.

As the evening progressed, Scarlett's sisters, along with Bekah, worked together to provide plenty of entertainment. There were several speeches and toasts as well as games, the latter of which culminated in a version of the Newlywed Game. To everyone's surprise, Devin remained in the lead for most of the contest. He knew the answers to every question, including Scarlett's shoe size and what she wore on their first date. Scarlett, however, won in the end with a "winner takes all" question where she guessed Devin's favorite pizza topping (mushrooms).

When it came time for the bouquet toss, all the single women gathered on the dance floor, with Emerald and Bekah at the forefront of the group.

"Who should I throw this to?" Scarlett asked Devin as he stood off to the side.

"Anyone but Bekah," he replied, semi-jokingly. "She's much too young to be thinking about marriage."

"I heard that, Dev! I'm a grown woman, for crying out loud." Bekah stuck her tongue out in protest.

"And you just proved my point," he countered with a shake of his head. "Enjoy your single life, sis. Relationships aren't as easy as you think they are."

"Ahem! *I* heard that!" Scarlett shot him a stern look that soon turned into a grin. "Your brother's right, Bekah. Relationships aren't easy, but they're worth it, aren't they, Dev?"

"You're absolutely right, sweetheart." Devin nodded and pretended to catch the kiss Scarlett blew his way. At the same moment, Jace walked past them, his expression one of wide-eyed disbelief. "What's that look for, Jace?"

"I have no idea who you are anymore, bro! I don't know how you did it, Scarlett," Jace exclaimed. "You've turned my brother into a big ball of mush."

"It's called the power of love. You'll experience it someday, and then the two of you can be big balls of mush together!"

Jace held his hands up as he backed away. "I'm good, thanks. I've got more than enough love from my adoring fans."

"You're missing out, brother," Devin remarked. "The love of a woman who knows you inside and out can change your life."

"Guys! We're not getting any younger here!" Emerald called out over the din of high-pitched voices urging Scarlett to throw the bouquet. "Any day now, Red!"

"All right, I'm on it!" Turning her back to the crowd, Scarlett counted down, "Three, two, one," then tossed the bouquet in the air. Instead of aiming it at the eager group of women, she threw it in the opposite direction. "Heads up, Jace!"

In the blink of an eye, Jace looked over and caught the red roses with one hand. "Seriously?"

Scarlett shrugged with a cheeky smile. "My hand slipped!" She then gave Devin a victorious smile as several of the single ladies rushed over to introduce themselves to Jace.

Devin walked over to his bride and kissed her on the cheek. "Well played, sweetheart. I'm afraid though that our sisters aren't too happy with your decision to give the bouquet to Jace."

She winced when she spotted the frowns on Emerald's and Bekah's faces. "I think Bekah will forgive me when I tell her I was only trying to keep her big brother off her case. As for Em—oh, look! Who's that cute guy she's talking to?"

"Cute guy?" Devin relaxed when he saw the man in question. "That's my cousin Joe, Nick's brother."

"Oh no. I should warn her about him!"

He took ahold of Scarlett's hand to stop her from running off.

Knowing how passionate his wife was, his cousin wouldn't stand a chance against her. "Joe's a good guy. He's not like Nick at all. Emerald will be fine. Besides, he'll find out soon enough that we've got our eyes on him."

"You bet we do!"

Scarlett's feisty tone started him chuckling. "Why do I get the feeling that I need to watch my back, too?"

"Don't worry, I've got my eyes on you, too, but for different reasons." She winked.

Later on, as the festivities began to wind down, Jace and his band played covers of popular love songs for those still on the dance floor. Devin cradled Scarlett in his arms as the two of them got lost in their own world in a corner of the ballroom. He rested his chin on the top of her head, breathing in her delicate floral scent and marveling at how well they moved in sync. They may have started out on opposing sides, but they had grown to appreciate and support one another. No one other than Scarlett could bring out the best in him. He was a fortunate man, blessed beyond belief. Who would have imagined that he would be married before year's end? Certainly not him. But God had better plans than he ever could have put together on his own.

"You're awfully quiet, Mr. CEO," Scarlett remarked, pulling back to see him. She looked breathtakingly beautiful with her hair pulled back in a low bun. The pearl and diamond earrings she wore, which once belonged to his mother, suited her well. She tipped her head to one side as she studied him. "What are you thinking about? Let me guess—you can't wait to wear your new froggy pjs later, am I right?"

"Close." He grinned. "I was thinking about how nice it is to have someone to share my life with."

"Someone or me?" She wrinkled her nose in chagrin. "There's a difference, you know. I hope you mean me."

"Of course. I doubt if there's any other woman who'd put up with me and my sparkling personality."

Scarlett burst out with a laugh. "You're a lot funnier than you give yourself credit for, Devin Kendall."

"I believe my sense of humor only came out after I met you. You changed my life for the better, sweetheart."

"As you did for me." She smoothed down the lapels of his tuxedo and smiled wistfully. "And to think that I'd once thought of you as a grump, and we didn't get along. I'm so glad I got to know you better."

"It took a while, but you've finally come to your senses," he teased. "I just happened to come to mine faster."

"I don't know about that. Need I remind you that I kissed you first?"

"But I was the one who proposed first."

Scarlett rolled her eyes. "All right, I give in. You win."

Shaking his head, he pulled her close. "No, we both win. There are no losers in this game of love. You and I win because we're in this together."

"You're so right. We're in this together," she echoed. "How'd you get so smart?"

"They say two heads are better than one. It must be your influence."

She grinned. "I knew you had a good sense of humor, Devin Kendall. Pair that with my brain, and we'll be unstoppable."

"I like the sound of that. There's no one else I'd rather win with than you, Scarlett Kendall."

"Scarlett Kendall—I really love the sound of that."

Devin did, too. He didn't know what the future held, but he knew that as long as they held onto the Lord and to each other, he and Scarlett would be as she said—unstoppable.

That was one truth he would gladly hold onto for the rest of their lives.

Afterword

Thank you so much for reading Devin and Scarlett's story! I hope you enjoyed meeting them!

When I was thinking of a new series to write, I immediately decided to center it on a family. I love the dynamics that siblings have and believe that birth order makes a big difference in one's personality, beliefs, and behaviors. Since I'd already written a series about brothers, I wanted to include a sister in this one. I also wanted to have a set of twins in the family because I've always been fascinated with twins. So, that's how the Kendall family came to be.

I drew a lot of inspiration for this story from the C-dramas that I watch, which usually feature an alpha male CEO. I just love it when a guy who appears stoic and in control on the outside totally melts and softens up when he meets the quirky and lovable girl who makes him smile. That's how I imagined Devin feeling when Scarlett entered his world and turned it upside down. LOL. I also love it when a guy accepts a girl for who she is and doesn't want

AFTERWORD

her to change, just like Devin did with Scarlett. I think they're a perfect match, don't you?

Thanks again for reading *Saving the CEO*! I'd appreciate it if you would leave your honest review and let me know what you thought of the story!

Also, if you're curious to know what Devin and Scarlett are up to now, I have an update for you over on my website (liwenho.com)! Check out Issue #1 of my *Lovebug Letters* magazine HERE.

* * *

If you love books featuring siblings, be sure to check out my Spark Brothers series!

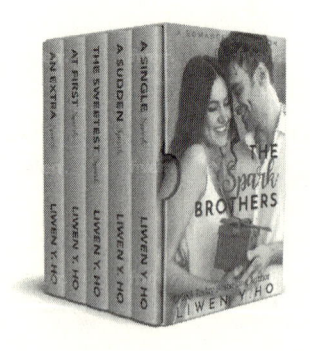

In this charming collection of Christian romances, meet the five handsome Spark brothers — and the women who capture their hearts! A sweet box set filled with faith, love, and family.

Why reviewers love the Spark brothers:
"These Spark brothers sure do set a girl's heart on fire."

AFTERWORD

"I absolutely LOVE this series. This is an awesome family of five brothers all who have a strong faith."

"I know I enjoy books when they feel real and after this series, I wish the Spark brothers were real. Thank you, Liwen Y. Ho, for writing stories to remind me that God wastes nothing and is always at work. Now please excuse me while I go reread the series."

A Single Spark (Book One): A pop singer running from his past. A deejay who's given up on men. Will the sparks igniting between them end up in flames or romance?

A Sudden Spark (Book Two): A writer too shy to speak to women. A single mom who's sworn off men. Will a marriage of convenience end their friendship or spark a lasting romance?

The Sweetest Spark (Book Three): A fun-loving ice cream shop owner looking for more than a fling. A straight-laced food critic too scared for love. Will an accident be the spark that drives them apart for good or gives them their sweetest taste of romance yet?

At First Spark (Book Four): A tender-hearted firefighter who's been burned by love. An optimistic bookstore owner determined to heal his heart. Will the spark that drew them to each other be enough to keep their love burning or will their short-lived romance go down in flames?

An Extra Spark (Book Five): An actor pressured to risk everything for his job. An actress struggling to fit into the Hollywood scene. Will the hazards of show business spark new insecurities or strengthen their bond of trust?

You can grab all 5 books as one box set HERE!

Acknowledgments

I'd like to thank the following people who blessed me in the making of this book:

My Lord and Savior for saving me and loving me just as I am, but also being patient with me as I learn and grow.

My hubby and our two munchkins for teaching me all about the dynamics of firstborn kids vs younger siblings.

My amazing proofreader Regina Dowling for catching all my errors and making all the right suggestions for this manuscript. Please don't retire anytime soon! ;)

My critique partners, Jocelynn and Kristen, for being my cheerleaders through all the ups and downs of writing this book.

My wonderful Lovebugs from my reader group who gave me so many great suggestions for this story and for their never-ending encouragement and support!

My awesome ARC readers for taking time out of their busy schedules to help launch this book baby into the world.

You, dear reader, for taking a chance on this new story and series!

About the Author

Liwen Y. Ho works as a chauffeur and referee by day (AKA being a stay at home mom) and an author by night. She writes sweet and inspirational contemporary romance infused with heart, humor, and a taste of home (her Asian roots).

In her pre-author life, she received a Master's degree in Marriage and Family Therapy from Western Seminary, and she loves makeovers of all kinds, especially those of the heart and mind. She lives in the San Francisco Bay Area with her techie husband and their two children.

Sign up for Liwen's newsletter to receive an exclusive free book, news about her upcoming releases, giveaways, sneak peeks, and more at: http://liwenho.com/free-book.

Also by Liwen Y. Ho

Fab Forties Series
Retying the Knot
Head Over Stilettos
Joined at the Hip
Love at Second Sight

Edenvale Arts Academy Series
How to Kiss a Guy in Ten Days
To the Only Boy I've Loved Before
While You Were Flirting
The Perks of Being a Rebel
Ten Things I Like About You

Heroes of Freedom Ridge Series
Love Pact with the Hero
Romanced by the Hero
Second Chance with the Hero

Sage Valley Ranch Series
Adored by the Cowboy

Lawkeepers Series
Lawfully Cherished

The Spark Brothers Series

A Single Spark
A Sudden Spark
The Sweetest Spark
At First Spark
An Extra Spark

Billionaires with Heart Series
At Odds with the Billionaire
Best Friends with the Billionaire
Crushing on the Billionaire

Taking Chances on Love Series
Taking a Chance on the Heartbreaker
Taking a Chance on Mr. Wrong
Taking a Chance on the Enemy

Seasons of Love Series
The More the Merrier
A Spoonful of Spice
Of Buds and Blossoms
On Waves of Wanderlust

Tropical Kiss Series
Tropical Kiss or Miss
Tropical Kiss and Tell

Welcome To Romance Series
Chasing Romance
Romantically Ever After

Holding Onto Love in Romance

Non-Series Books
Puppy Dog Tales
The Love Clause
Second Chance Sweethearts
The Time Rift (co-authored with David H. Ho)

Made in the USA
Columbia, SC
22 December 2024